An Impossible LOVE STORY

Ellie Hall

ABOUT THIS BOOK

Colette has a serious case of FOMO. Antonio's motto is YOLO. When their paths cross could it be ILU forever?

This is supposed to be a summer to remember as I work my way through Europe with a bucket list I hoped would give me closure. But when I get stranded, neither my southern charm nor my sassy mouth can talk me out of trouble.

Except when trouble is tall, dark, and Italian...a handsome heartthrob, a hero, a hottie. Kidding. That's the sweltering heat going to my head. I'll just go grab another gelato to cool off.

However, the list repeatedly leads me to Antonio. Well, the bucket list and the love list—a silly thing my friends packed in my luggage, claiming that when I found a guy that met the criteria, I'd also fall in love.

I didn't have the guts to tell them that I'm not looking. They don't know about my past. However, it turns out that I am a sucker for adventures along quaint cobblestone streets, coins tossed in fountains, and a certain pair of brown eyes. That love list? Check, check, and check.

When Antonio tells me the way he feels, there's no need to translate. The thing is, I feel the same way. But do I dare risk my heart again and take a detour that might mean HEA?

NOTE TO READER

My family and I planned to go to Europe last summer after my daughter's high school graduation, to visit some family, and for an Irish dance competition. Yes, we would've been busy! It also would've been their first time overseas.

While I've been to many of the places Colette and Antonio visit *in An Impossible Love Story*, I was filled with anticipation and excitement about seeing the sites through their eyes.

Unfortunately, I wasn't able to share the traveling experience with them at that time. However, through writing this story, I created a love letter of my own to travel. Also, in a way, I'm able to show them some sights without leaving home. I hope you can too and find a delightful moment of escape on these pages—along with laughter because poor Colette is a mermaid out of water until she finds her Romeo.

Yep, I'm mixing idioms and symbols there, but like when on the road, we'll just roll with it.

Happy reading!

Ellie

P.S. Please note any errors or changes in travel details, customs, etcetera are my own. I was working from memory and photographs.

CHAPTER 1
EAT, PRAY, LEAP!
COLETTE

I'm not crying. My eyes are just leaking. Is there a plumber for this kind of thing?

It isn't fair to feel grief so dense on such a sunny day. It's summer. I should be outside, at least.

My phone beeps with a text.

I startle and quickly stash the piece of paper under my pillow as if I'm a teenager and my mother came in and caught me looking at something naughty. Not that I would. I'm a southern girl. As proper as they come.

Minnie's name appears in the little bubble.

Minnie: Come meet me. It's a beautiful day. You should be outside.

Like I said.

Me: How do you know I'm not outside?

Minnie: I was just imitating a nagging parent, dragging you out of bed.

She isn't wrong...I am still in bed, but I'm definitely no longer a teenager even though my thoughts and heart feel trapped in time. I glance at the digital clock. Let's not even talk about what time it is.

Me: Okay, Mom. What should I do outside? Have any chores that need doing?

Minnie: Ha ha. Meet me for iced coffee and we'll take a whimsy.

Me: A what?

In response, she takes a selfie in front of our favorite coffee shop.

Peppy, positive people encourage you to seize the day. Lately, for me, it's more like *snooze the day*. I used to be one of them, grabbing life by the horns and doing all the things plus ten more.

I drag myself to my feet. As I pass the floor-length mirror, I give a lazy salute. Then wrinkle my nose.

Marcus would hardly recognize me. Is this what he'd want? Broken Colette? Sad Colette? Crying Colette?

I don't dare answer that question because the girl he knew and loved was bubbly Colette. Sparkly Colette. Cheerful Colette.

And I was. For a long time, I bucked up and crushed life. I excelled in school, top of my class. I'm bilingual—*bonjour*! I could probably ace a calculus exam if I sat down to take one, even though it's been twelve years since I graduated. Okay, okay. Maybe not calc. But I can still recite Shakespeare fluently.

My physics teacher suggested an engineering track for me. Instead, I studied law and passed the bar on the first try. That was the plan, and I stuck to it even if life didn't turn out like I expected.

All of this is to say, I'm smart and not ashamed of it. However, none of that prepared me for how to handle this sadness that follows me out the door of my building. I'd bucked up, but now I'm just buckling under this weight that's getting heavier by the day.

No one warned me that over ten years in, grief can still be sticky. Kind of like Manhattan in the summer. Minnie said it's beautiful outside. More like humid and that's saying something, considering I'm originally from South Carolina.

The armpits of my shirt are soggy and I have five blocks to

go. I should've worn a tank top. Or stayed in bed with the air conditioning and plenty of tissues.

The AC at the café we dubbed *Dude Taco's Dad's Coffee Emporium* welcomes me. We also call it *Man Bun Barista's Beanery* and the *Dating Dare Café*—a long and funny story, but I digress. It's actually called *Forty-Nine West* because it's on the west side of Manhattan and located on Forty-Ninth Street. The owner, Bash, wasn't too creative on that front. But his coffee, croissants, and pastries are divine.

My eyes itch. Nope. Not allergies. It's the croissants, I swear. Thankfully, I can eat gluten all day every day, but it's the memory attached to croissants and why I took French in high school that gets me. Gets me all the time lately.

Minnie waves me over, seated at our usual table. Catherine won't set foot in here, but the rest of us keep tabs on Bash for Book Boyfriend Blog purposes.

Not that I'm looking for a boyfriend. No sir-ee. But my best girlfriends don't know that. No ma'am.

Minnie dives in, talking a mile a minute.

"Wait. What?" I glance at the empty espresso cup. "How many of those have you had?"

"You took ages to get here."

"It's not easy to look this good." My beauty pageant winner grandmama would be rolling over in her grave if she saw me in this state. No full face. No lip liner. No glue-on lashes. Mascara and gloss are enough for me.

"I had the idea to be a tourist in the city this summer. For instance, have you ever been to the top of the Empire State Building?" Minnie asks.

I tip my head from side to side. "No. As a matter of fact, I haven't."

"See? There's so much to do right here." She goes on, citing more places to visit.

The *list* comes to mind. The one I was looking at when Minnie texted. Paris, London, Amsterdam...

"All this right in our backyard." Minnie's excitement pulls me from my drizzly thoughts. "So I started to make an itinerary. A bunch of places to visit."

Just then the scent of perfume and the sound of melodious laughter echoes from the doorway.

Hazel never fails to make an entrance. She sees us immediately and struts over. Maxwell gets in line to place their order.

Taking a seat, she says, "It's Sunday. We should be having brunch. Wait. You don't have anything to eat or drink, Colette." She leans closer to me. "You've been looking a little thin lately." Then she calls, "Maxwell, please make it two. So what are we talking about?"

This woman operates her own power station. I used to have that kind of oomph and energy. My sigh sounds like it belongs to an elephant.

"Being tourists in the city this summer," Minnie exclaims like it's the greatest idea ever.

Hazel agrees. Maxwell comes over and the conversation turns toward travel.

I zone out as I pick at the jumbo blueberry muffin Maxwell got me.

"I have travel points that are about to expire. Too bad they don't transfer to museum admission," he says. Not that he has to worry about money.

Me neither, at least for a little while. I haven't told them that I took a little hiatus from work. It's been three weeks.

Nope. I haven't gotten bored yet in case you're wondering. Sleeping all day can keep boredom at bay.

"Have you ever been?" Hazel asks.

I blink a few times. "What? Been where?"

Hazel discretely flashes Minnie a look of concern. About me. I want to tell them, *Ladies, you don't have to worry about me. This is a little blip, a rut. It'll pass.* But I don't say the words because they're weak. Because I'm not so sure they're true. I haven't been to work in three weeks, but I've felt this low for months. It's not getting better.

"Have you been to Europe? There was that Belgian fella..." Hazel waggles her eyebrows.

"Who?" Then I remember the guy from Brussels that I briefly dated. Well, if showing him to the post office on Forty-Third Street and asking him about waffles and chocolate counts. I was going there anyway, and the line was long. We talked for a while. My thoughts muddle and meld. "No, never been to Europe. We were going to for our twenty-first birthdays, but—"

When the confusion on Minnie, Hazel, and Maxwell's faces registers, I realize I've said all of this out loud.

"Who?" Minnie asks, echoing my question from about two minutes back.

"We, um—" When I was a little girl, I broke my mother's favorite coffee mug. I hid it in the laundry basket. For three days, I lived in fear of waking up to her hollering at me in a caffeine-deprived state.

I jumped at the gurgle of the coffee maker. Every night when I said my prayers, I almost confessed. Then on that third day, when she got around to doing laundry and asked me what the mug was doing there and why it was broken, my brain created no less than five lies on the spot. But the truth had been preparing its number, polishing its shoes. It tap-danced its way out of my mouth.

My mom placed her arm around me and thanked me for telling her the truth and that next time I ought to do so right away. She also said that she didn't like the idea of the cup sitting in a heap with dad's underwear. We both laughed. The truth felt good.

But right now, it terrifies me. My brain concocts no less than five stories to tell my friends, but it also still recalls its love for shiny patent leather, the click-click of the metal taps on the wooden stage...and the freeing feeling of laughter.

"We. Marcus and me. My high school sweetheart." A sniffle starts, but I force it away.

"Is that the guy who won you the jar of chocolate kisses at the sweetheart dance?" Minnie asks, referring to our Galentine's Day party when I mentioned that story sans details.

"Then gave you that many kisses." Hazel's accurate recollection makes my heart dip.

Back around Valentine's Day, I was cleaning out my closet to donate a bunch of stuff to charity and came across a box.

The do-not open Pandora's kind of box. The one that contained all the physical evidence of my broken heart.

You can guess what I did.

The lid came off. Hasn't gone back on.

The overwhelming desire to run away came and hasn't left. Not run away from home—I've already moved out—, but from this grief, sitting on my chest, clawing at my skin, and gnawing on my bones.

Not run away so much as to disappear to *disapparate*—like in Harry Potter. The geeky film spots in London were one of the places I put on the bucket list but secretly knew that Marcus wanted to visit too.

"You and Marcus?" Hazel repeats carefully, as if she senses this is hallowed territory.

"He was my high school sweetheart. We started dating early junior year. We were instant best friends after I broke into the football field snack bar, spent the night popping popcorn, and then filled up the teacher's lounge with it."

Maxwell chortles. "So sly. A teenage mastermind."

"Mwah ha ha." I twiddle my fingers.

"So you guys were going to Europe when you turned twenty-one?" Minnie asks.

"We'd made a bucket list—or wish list—of a bunch of places we wanted to visit and had a shoebox and would put money in it to save up. I still have the four hundred and ten dollars we saved. It was going to be our honeymoon."

"You were going to get married?" Hazel coos. "That's so sweet."

And that's when the curtain comes down. The show is over. I tiptoe in my tap shoes off the stage. The thing is, we did get married, but I can't tell them that. Or what happened later. It's too painful.

"High school romance. Tale as old as time. You mean to keep in touch while going to different colleges. Too bad it rarely works out," Bash says from a crouch on the floor.

I startle. We all turn to look at the coffee shop owner with his man bun.

"How long were you standing there?" I ask. "Er, squatting."

"I was adjusting this table." He jiggles it with his hand. "Customers keep complaining that it's wobbly." He smiles thinly. "It's not the table. It's the floor. They should be complaining that these old boards are uneven." Turning on his heel, he huffs off.

"I am so thankful Catherine didn't end up with him," Minnie whispers.

Hazel bats her hand. "He's nice in a quirky kind of way."

I eye our surroundings, worried he may have heard that too. But he's back by the register.

Hazel lights up. "Colette, you should use Maxwell's travel points and go to Europe. Make good on that bucket-wish list. Can she use them?" she says as if Bash's assumption was correct that my high school sweetheart and I went our separate ways in college and broke up.

Maxwell smiles. "Of course. We racked them up during our honeymoon and aren't going to have a chance to use them before they expire."

"You can take selfies and post them on social, telling that Marcus guy he's missing out." Minnie cackles like happiness is the best revenge. She'd be right, but I'm not seeking revenge. More like healing.

Hazel bounces in her seat. "And we'll make you a love list.

Wouldn't it be ironic if you met the love of your life while on a trip that you were supposed to go on with the bucket list bozo?"

I already took off the tap shoes. I don't correct her. Marcus wasn't a bozo. He was the best.

"Okay, so where's the list? What's the itinerary?" Hazel rubs her hands together. She lives for this kind of thing.

Without thinking, I pull it out of my purse.

Hazel reads, "London, Amsterdam, Copenhagen, Stockholm, and Paris."

"Marcus wanted to see where his Scandinavian ancestors came from—he had a Viking obsession. My picks were London and Paris."

"You'll be closer to Catherine," Minnie muses.

Okay, I'll admit, I'm kind of zoned out. A bit numb at exposing part of the truth about my past that I've kept tucked away during the decade-plus of our friendship.

The girls make a list of quintessential European experiences —cobblestone streets, wishes in fountains, and ample amounts of pastries. They call it the *Love List*.

Minnie's cheeks turn pink when Hazel mentions Tyler's usual trip to France for the holidays.

However, they don't know what really happened to Marcus and why I've embellished about the dating I've done since we've been friends. Granted, I've gone on a few real dates and "seen" guys for weeks or a month, tops. But no one ever compared to Marcus, so why bother?

But I snap back to focus when I hear them discussing departure times.

"I can't just pick up and leave," I say.

"What's stopping you?" Hazel asks.

"You're not working on a case," Minnie adds.

"How do you—?"

"I stopped by the office last week to surprise you with lunch," Minnie says. "Elsa said you're on leave for the summer."

She slaps the table. "I just thought of something. Are you pregnant?"

My brow furrows. "No." I'd have to be involved with someone for that to happen. Not to mention married. I don't want grandmama to curse me.

Hazel scans me again, highlighting the fact that I probably have lost a little weight. "No. She's not pregnant. It's not like we haven't noticed, Colette. You're our best friend. You're in a funk. You need to shake things up."

Maxwell, new to our group but not to my friends' antics, fidgets, slightly uncomfortable at the personal turn the conversation has taken.

You and me both, brother.

Minnie flashes her phone at me, showing off travel social media accounts she follows with quirky names like *WanderLost* and *Seek, Find, Float.* "Oh, check out this one. *From Europe with a Kiss.*"

"Ooh, he's cute," Hazel says, pointing at a picture of a guy from that last account, which features famous destinations with accidental photobombs of attractive European men in the background.

She's not wrong, but I'm not looking for attractive European, or Manhattan, men for that matter.

Maxwell grunts.

Hazel kisses his cheek. "Not as cute as you, babe."

I twist a napkin around my finger. "I like Minnie's touring Manhattan idea better."

"Nope. You'll get a confirmation email for your plane ticket." Hazel sets Maxwell's phone down. "JFK to Heathrow tomorrow."

I tuck my chin back and shake my head. "Hazel, no. I can't go to Europe tomorrow."

"It's first-class, darling."

"No way. What about accommodations and the nine-million other details?"

Hazel taps away on her phone. "I'll arrange everything. My friend Jesse will meet you too. You'll have the best time. It'll be an unforgettable experience. A summer to remember."

"I can't go to Europe by myself."

"But your eighty-two-year-old grandmother went to Alaska, alone. *Alaska.* Think about that."

"It is the final frontier," Maxwell says.

No, that's space, but I keep the correction to myself because I don't want them to get any crazy ideas.

I sag in my seat. "It was the only state she'd never visited."

"Sounds like bucket list material to me," Hazel singsongs.

Minnie cocks her head slightly, leveling me with a *think-about-that-carefully* look. "If your grandmama can visit Alaska solo, surely you can tour Europe."

I hedge, squirming in my seat.

"When was the last time you went on vacation?" Maxwell asks after Hazel gives him a not-so-subtle look to back her up.

"Three, four years ago. I've been busy at the firm. Socking away money for a rainy day." I wince. "A rainy day being retirement."

"It rains a lot in England," Hazel says knowingly, since that's where she's from. She leans in. "Think about it like this. You're burned out, depressed, you're single, and it's summer."

"Wow. You really know how to make a lady feel good," I mutter.

"It'll be a soul journey. Your very own E*at, Pray, Love,*" Minnie adds.

"Sounds dramatic. More like Eat, Pray, Leap into the unknown," I grumble.

But they won't hear any more of my protests or objections.

And that, my friends, is how I end up on a red-eye to London. With red eyes. From crying. Unforgettable? More like unbelievable.

Hazel and Minnie lead me to the security checkpoint at the

airport. The guard gives me a stern, "Move along" when I refuse to let go of them.

"It's not like we're forcing her to get an MRI or a pelvic exam," Minnie mutters.

"It's not like you're about to go on holiday to Europe." Hazel's expression is pure sarcasm.

"By myself," I say. That was not part of the original bucket list plan.

They pause as if considering whether sending me out of the country in this state is wise.

"Nope. We have to do this quick and dirty, like tearing off a bandage," Hazel says, shrugging me off.

It's then I realize the trip to the coffee shop was an intervention. "It's not fair. It's two against one. If Catherine weren't in Italy and Lottie in love, they'd have my back."

"When I told Catherine, she encouraged it, extended her stay so you could visit."

I sink back as travelers brush past me, clearly annoyed, but whoosh me into their midst. *New Yorkers. Sheesh.*

My best friends wave and blow kisses as I'm sucked through security and into the unknown.

CHAPTER 2
I'M NO ROMEO
ANTONIO

The mist off the sea crawls along the tracks. My damp hair tickles my forehead. The diffuse light from the train headlight glows closer and I board, glancing over my shoulder in goodbye, but I can't see anything beyond the few inches in front of me through the fog.

Seems like the opening for a horror movie, but this just an early morning in Scotland during the summer.

Once seated, my eyes dip closed as I leave the way I arrived. Spring came and went, bringing me no closer to answers.

I doze, but my head jostles against the window, repeatedly startling me awake. We trundle past the backs of sleeping houses, nestled under a never-ending gray blanket.

How I miss the glorious sunshine. I'm not horror movie material. More like a musical, but lately, I've been moody like this weather. Then again, my father would rather have me play the role of a mob boss…er, a mob boss in training.

I began the search for my mother in Italy and have been all over Europe, most recently in Glasgow and now back to London.

When I step into the now-familiar station, an elderly man reads the newspaper. A businesswoman sips coffee, talks on the phone, and types and swipes on her tablet. A mother tows a toddler behind her. The flecks of mica in the floor fascinate the little boy. My heart tugs at an imagined memory, my mother leading me by the hand through the train station—instead of leaving me.

Doubt creeps in. Surrounded by people striding past with determination and purpose, my resolve crinkles and seems somewhat flimsy. What am I really doing, anyway?

Good question.

For a while now, when there's a knock on the door, I think it's her. When I get an unexpected call, I think she's finally contacting me. When I see a crowd part, I expect her to appear. Part of me knows she isn't coming and what I'm feeling, deep in my stomach, is disappointment. Still, I envision our reunion, of me finding her, what I'll say, how we'll hug, and how everything will be better.

But will it?

Like the oldest buildings in Italy, I've reinforced my exterior in stone, so sentiment doesn't have a chance to render me into sediment.

My stomach growls as I pass fast-food joints and a few healthier options offering salads and smoothies.

I could go for a burger with extra cheese, but it's a bit early in the day.

I take the Piccadilly line toward London proper. Even though a train is a train, whether in New York or England, the energy inside this carriage, with its blue seats and red accents, is more polite, for one. But it also carries the air of a place waking up, or perhaps that's just me. Except for the shushing of the train, the Tube is quiet as the world streaks by. Each time we stop at a familiar station: Hammersmith, Gloucester Road, and Knightsbridge. My pulse increases with excitement, anticipation.

I love the high vibe of a city. If I weren't a tall, intimidating looking Italian, I might possibly burst into song. The English probably wouldn't approve. The tourists would be terrified. Someone would cart me off.

I keep my hands clasped and my mouth closed.

Being back here, hope returns. Like I'm back on the right trail, getting closer to my mother—it's like the childhood game, hot and cold. When getting closer to a hidden thing, the person says *hotter*. If you're far away, they say *colder*. Or for me, in Italian, it would be *caldo* or *freddo*.

The smooth voice of the announcement for Piccadilly Circus comes over the speakers. Instinct whispers, *hotter*. This is where I'll get off. It's as though I feel her near.

The blare of horns and the flashing neon signs at street level remind my throbbing head that I haven't slept properly in a few nights.

My stomach guides me toward the familiar scent of frying dough. I pop into a café, order a cappuccino, and feast my eyes on the creative takes on traditional doughnuts in the display case. They remind me of the semester I spent in America. I order a vanilla bean doughnut glazed with chocolate and sprinkled with hazelnuts—they all have funky names like *Red velvet goldmine*, *Crème de la crème*, and *Better than a kiss*. That's the one I get with a chocolate candy kiss nestled in the center.

I take a seat by a fountain and am ready to bite into the fluffy, delicious melt-in-my mouth confection, but a motion by the winged sculpture of the Greek god Eros atop the fountain catches my attention. I glance back at my doughnut. As far I'm concerned, this might be love. The motion turns into commotion and I turn all the way around.

A petite woman with long blond hair piled in a mess on top of her head and holding a doughnut like mine mounts the wall on the fountain and angles her phone, trying to capture the doughnut, the statue, and herself in the frame. She tilts the device, leans to one side, and then the other before shaking her head with frustration.

"See what you're missing?" she mutters in an American accent—southern, I think.

Just then, her arms windmill. She clutches her phone, but the doughnut sails out of her hands, landing in the fountain like a little pool float.

She lunges for the doughnut, loses her footing, and tips toward the water. I race forward with my arms outstretched. I belatedly realize it looks like I'm rushing at her, ready to smash her face with the chocolate doughnut like a cream pie in a slapstick comedy movie.

She lurches to the side and sends the pigeons scattering. We both land on the ground. She on her side and me on my stomach. Somehow I managed to keep the doughnut aloft.

I glance up at her dark eyes, the color of espresso, my favorite drink. They're a contrast to her blond hair. A smattering of brown freckles spread from her nose to her cheeks. Her lips are perfectly proportioned and heart-shaped.

"Ciao," I say. "We could've used Eros' wings there." I offer a half-smile.

"Huh?" she asks, sitting up and brushing off her hands.

"Are you okay?"

"No. My friends kidnapped me. Put me on a plane. Jet lag. Tired." A forlorn sigh escapes. "And I lost my doughnut." She frowns at it floating in the water. "It looked so good."

"Here you can have mine."

She carefully looks me up and down like I'm a flat—an apartment to Americans—and she's deciding if she wants to rent it or not. I fight the urge to tell her I'm not for lease. Not available. Not attached either, but not looking for love. No, I'm looking for my mother. Another kind of love altogether.

"That's mighty kind of you, sir, But no thank you. I don't know where those hands of yours have been."

"Berlin, Vienna, Brussels, Prague, South of France. Most recently Glasgow. Before that Edinburgh. You could say I have travel fever or itchy feet."

She wrinkles her nose as if not understanding what I mean.

"I've traveled quite a lot. I was saying where my hands have been. I took the train back to London just today." Maybe it's too early in the morning to joke around.

I extend my hand to help her to her feet.

When she doesn't immediately reach for to grasp my hand, I say, "Don't worry. It's not contagious. At least I don't think so."

Her eyes dart from side to side and then travel up my length again as if uncertain whether I have hand-foot-mouth disease.

When her fingers do connect with mine, there's softness and warmth. Nothing gritty or cold like the stone urban streets.

As I draw her up, momentum thrusts her forward and she's close enough I inhale her scent—like magnolias on a fresh summer morning. Like this morning.

Her face falls and she shuffles back. "There, now your hands have been to South Carolina." The words come slow, hesitant as though she doesn't mean to say them.

I tilt my head. "Is that where you're from?"

"I arrived from New York City at an hour I'd like to delete from the clock, but before that a small town outside Charleston, South Carolina. So have I traveled much? No, I have not. And I've probably lost my marbles. *Rule number one in solo travel, don't tell anyone you've just fallen off the turnip truck...or that you're traveling alone.* Okay. I'm going to be on my way now. Thanks for trying to break my fall. Cheerio." She winces and then rushes off.

She lost her what? I hurry after her. "Excuse me, miss? What do you mean you lost your marbles off the turnip truck?" My English isn't perfect, but I pride myself on having a passable understanding of the language, at least enough to work here in London, but I cannot fathom what she just said.

"It's a turn of phrase. Rather, two, but you twisted them up. Lost my marbles means I lost my mind. Falling off the turnip truck means naïve or easily fooled. English Lesson 101 with Professor Clark is now over. You may leave the classroom."

I look around then realize she's joking and give her a full smile, wagging my finger. "Now, I understand. Please, let me buy you a doughnut in exchange for being such a great tutor."

"Ha. Nice try, Romeo. I know all about swarthy, charming, heartbreakers like you. Nope. This turnip truck is moving on. Ciao."

I call after her, "I'm Antonio, actually. My father's name is Romeo. Though everyone calls him Ro." I almost managed not to say the name with disdain.

She wiggles her fingers in a friendly wave but her expression says *we're done here.*

I watch the slight sway of her hips as she leaves. Another pretty woman, gone from my life. Not that they ever stick around. I've learned that lesson multiple times over.

The doughnut is a little worse for wear and smooshed around the edge, but I take a bite and return to my coffee, still perched on the side of the fountain. The pulse of London pumps through me, the caffeine rockets in my veins, the midmorning sun warms me, and I am on a mission.

I amble around Piccadilly for a little while before turning onto Regent Street. The British flag hangs overhead as I follow the old, curving road, coming alive with pedestrians and cars. I pass shops and boutiques, restaurants, and pubs, but all I want to do is look up, up, up at the Georgian architecture. All of it is a photographer's dream. My camera comes out and I lose myself to the muse.

My wealth originally came from the family biz, but when I quit that, I've picked up odd jobs and am good at investing and saving. However, if I ever did pursue a university degree, the track options would be:

a) Take over the family business. This was the plan up until my brother exposed the fact that the woman I thought was my mother was not. Thanks for the lifelong lie, Papa.

b) Pursue photography. This is where my heart lives, but don't imagine my family would smile upon it. Not that I care. much. Up until recently, they were my life.

c) Look for my mother and hopefully find answers, figure out where I fit in, and put distance between myself and the feeling of betrayal.

After a while, I cross Pall Mall and into Waterloo Gardens. The first time I saw it, it was less grand than I expected. According to my mother's journal, the only connection I have to her, she loved flowers and wrote in her journal that she frequently visited the gardens in London. Perhaps not this one though. I pause and flip through the little notebook. There's no mention of Waterloo Gardens. However, highlights do include Westminster Abbey, Big Ben, Tower Bridge, among others. I've been to half the places she mentioned, looking, searching, hoping that I'll find something that will lead me to her.

I pass a few bums and toss them each a coin, wondering where their wandering hearts lead them and if they want to be wandering at all. There's a woman, laden in shawls even in the summer heat. She could be my mother. She's likely someone's mother. Will I know my own when I see her? Will she know me? I imagine her living in a little cottage and tending roses, with tea laid out as though she's been waiting for me all this time.

Cue the music and me singing a lonely tune.

I sniff an orange rose with pale white along the edges of the petals. It's thorny and neglected, but blooming nonetheless, I'm overcome with worry and a pang of loneliness. I leave it in the garden, but I take the scent of magnolia and moonlight with me. The fragrance of the woman by the fountain who called herself Professor Clark.

A smile slides across my face.

She was cute and made me laugh, but I'm not looking for cute. Rather, cozy and motherly, and maybe another doughnut. Or a pastry. That would do too.

CHAPTER 3
AMAZED AND CONFUSED
COLETTE

Let's address the fact that the guy who helped me out by the fountain looked a lot like the photo of the hottie on the account Minnie showed me called *From Europe with a Kiss*.

I'm suspicious and know better than to trust these foreign men with their alluring smiles, delicious scents, and charming accents.

Okay, the one man, but still. Antonio, I think he said his name was?

I'm not thinking about him. Nope. That would probably be the other women he tries to charm. (When I originally planned to go to Europe, Grandmama warned me about Italian men, Romeos she called them, and how'd they try to pinch my fanny. That's a butt for those of you who don't speak Grandmama.)

After circling a lake in a park, I emerge through the wrought-iron gates to a horseshoe of stately buildings. I vaguely remember learning about the significance of Whitehall when I did a report in geography class years ago, highlighting the parade during the Queen's Birthday—I wore Mama's home-coming crown when I did the presentation.

I cross the vast concrete, feeling small and lost. Pigeons pluck and peck about, not scattering when I get near like when I catapulted into a group of them after almost falling into the fountain. It was the water or the birds—I chose not to get wet.

"Sorry, guys," I mutter as I pass in case any of them were in the unlucky flock in Piccadilly.

Antonio, the guy who tried to break my fall and then offered me his doughnut hovers in my mind. Tall, tan, well-built. Brown hair. Brown eyes. Italian from head to toe.

Everything about him from his smile to the smolder to the fullness of his lips ticks off all the boxes in the *man candy* category.

There was nothing not to like. Everything about Antonio was perfect.

He came to my aid. Offered me food.

From across the pond, I can hear the collective shout of Catherine, Hazel, Lottie, and Minnie, asking me why I didn't chat with him longer or at least get his number.

I do have his name.

Antonio.

"Antonio," I whisper, mostly because I've only spoken to a bunch of pigeons in the last hour and not because I want to hear what it sounds like coming from my mouth.

"Not good, Colette. Not good."

I'm supposed to meet Hazel's friend Jesse, but she's a no-show. At least, I think it was supposed to be here. I turn in a circle. All the quaint cobblestone streets and old-world charm are starting to look the same. Despite having the smarts to turn on an international plan on my phone and the fact that I'm setting out on this stupid endeavor in an English-speaking country, something must've been lost in translation.

I guess I'm on my own. Thanks, Jesse.

Now, what to do? Where to go?

A group of tourists gathers for a photo and a few college-age people play an assortment of instruments and sing for spare change. Children visit one of the guard's horses, careful not to get too close.

A salesperson at a kiosk selling postcards, souvenirs, and maps of the city calls out, "Whatever you're looking for, we got it. Key chains, magnets, and mugs. Get all the goods here. We have what you need and more."

I try to slip by, keeping my head down. No eye contact. It works in Times Square on the rare and unfortunate occasions that I've passed through tourist central.

The portly guy calls, "Miss, whatcha looking for? I can help." He holds up a red telephone booth piggy bank in one hand and an umbrella with the British flag, though closed, in the other. I wave politely and stride past as if I have someplace important to go.

The second rule of travel: Don't engage with the junk vendors. Just keep on moving, girl.

I come close to not breaking it but then pause at the sound of a lilting Italian accent.

"I'm looking for my mother," he says to the salesman.

It's Romeo. I mean Antonio!

I pull out my phone so I blend in with the rest of the tourists taking photos. This isn't any of my business, but I can't help to discretely watch and listen.

The vendor's expression softens and his bushy eyebrows lift toward his bald head. "Well, there's an information desk inside the Cavalry Museum. Maybe try there, that's where separated tourists turn up. Though I suppose it's usually lost kids looking for their parents." He self-consciously pats his paunch, straining against his button-down shirt.

"Thanks." Antonio's a little too well-dressed to be one of those backpacker guys you hear about who couch surf around the world. But he doesn't scream *tourist* either.

I can't help wonder why he's looking for his mother if searching for her is what took him to all those places he listed when describing his itchy travel fever feet or whatever.

"I haven't seen her in thirty years," he says.

"Well, that's a different matter. Try missing persons?" the kiosk vendor suggests.

"No, it's not like that. She left." Antonio shrugs.

The man's bushy eyebrows pinch together. "Have you been drinking, mate?"

Antonio's chin tucks back. "No. I—" He shakes his head. "I had coffee and a doughnut. That's it."

"Do you need a drink, mate?" he asks, leaning back and changing tact.

Admittedly, it is an odd topic of conversation to strike up with a stranger. However, in Antonio's defense, the vendor did shout he had whatever anyone was looking for.

Antonio's eyebrows pinch together in adorable confusion.

The salesman says, "When I was younger sometimes a pint was a fitting solution to a problem. But I suppose when I lose something I retrace my steps. Go back to where I last saw what I lost."

"That's what I'm doing, sir. Sort of."

"I see then. Ah!" he exclaims, lifting a finger. "Do you have a map?"

"A journal." Antonio holds a slim diary.

He waves his hand dismissively and turns the carousel holding an assortment of maps. "Let's see. Yes, this one." He opens it up and holding it aloft with one hand, demonstrates how he'd systematically divide London into a grid and then canvas each section. "That way you're comprehensive, you get my meaning?"

Antonio buys the map and thanks the salesman. I return to the blank screen on my phone, pretending to be casually engrossed.

"When you find her, make sure you let me know that it all turned out. Maybe she'd like a commemorative mug or T-shirt," says the salesman.

"Ciao," Antonio replies, echoing the last thing I said to him.

A shadow crosses the gray light of the London morning. "Ciao," the voice repeats. Closer this time.

"Need a map?" Antonio asks. "How about a Big Ben key chain?" He puts it in my hand and like before when he helped me to my feet, I feel the rough buzz of connection, of longing. Of hands that have explored, touched the earth and maybe even the sky. "I insist," he says when I stand there, frozen…

Guilty.

Embarrassed.

Like a weirdo stalker.

I give my head a little shake because Antonio is even more handsome the second time. His eyes could make a girl melt. But not this southern girl. Nope. I'm reinforced with more than a few northeastern winters.

"Oh, Romeo. Funny to run into you again." I keep my voice flat but can't help wonder why he's looking for his mother. And how heartbreaking that is. Then again, I'm looking for something too. Just not sure what.

"No, I'm Antonio," he says as if I didn't tattoo his name in loopy cursive in my brain. "Professor South Carolina?"

"No, Colette Clark." I screw up my lips. But it's too late. *Rule number three of solo travel. Don't tell strangers your real name.*

His smolder radiates like the southern sun. "It's nice to meet you, Colette."

"Well, I should go check out Big Ben so I'm not cheating on being a proper tourist. Can't very well get a souvenir if I don't see the real McCoy." I waggle the key chain.

"The real Mc-what?"

"An expression. Never mind. Thanks and have a good day." The giant clock tower was not on the bucket list, but if I stay here a minute longer, I'm likely to break rule number four.

With a weak wave, I scamper off.

No, there isn't a rule number four unless you ask Minnie and Hazel. They gave me an overview of practical cautions to take when traveling abroad, but their biggest, juiciest, most frequently exclaimed rule was to hook up with a hottie.

Yes, those were their exact words. They'd be scolding me right now because Antonio definitely falls into that category.

But that is not why I'm here. I pull out the list Marcus and I made in high school. The ink is smudged, reminding me of a bruise. Like the one on my heart.

After I've been walking for another hour, I realize I'm on the other side of the park from before. I must have taken a wrong turn. The lake runs the length of the greenspace and I'm in the exact opposite place I meant to be. I should have used the map. I backtrack, annoyed and with an itchy layer of sticky sweat. My feet ache and a lump forms in my throat from the city air and frustration.

I continue toward the Thames, wondering what I expected.

Not to be here for one.

This wasn't my idea.

I pause mid-stride.

It wasn't my idea to get on a plane last night, but I'm an American. Land of the free. I could've dug in my heels. Told Hazel and Minnie I wasn't going to do it.

But for months, I've been taking that list out of the envelope like Bilbo and the ring in his pocket. *My secret. My precious.*

What do I want?

For Marcus to come back.

Not to be dead.

For our lives to have carried on as we'd planned.

Not to be a widow at eighteen.

For us to be here together.

Not to be alone.

It was a dangerous thing, but I brought a photo of him with me. It's tucked in the envelope too. I pull it out now and look at his toothy smile. His bright blue eyes. His Dutch boy hair cropped short.

The corners of my eyes pinch then liquify.

What did I expect, coming here?

Maybe I didn't expect anything and that's the problem. I sigh.

But I'm an American. Land of the free. Home of the brave.

Can I find the courage to do this?

The voice in my gut tells me that I have to. There's no other choice if I want to move forward.

I keep walking until the damp scent of freshwater tickles my nose. I turn a corner. At the end of the street, Big Ben looms, an arrow pointing toward the sky, keeping track of time so I don't have to.

Dwarfed by its majesty and reliability, I realize despite expectations and hopes, I have time on my side. There's nowhere that I need to be and nothing else I need to do. I have the rest of the summer to figure it out. The urgency that propelled me here skids and I stop. The clock chimes four times. My shoulders relax with relief, my jaw unclenches, and the velocity of the trip slows my pace as I continue toward the river.

I haven't eaten since the doughnut with the chocolate kiss in the center—I doubled back and got a replacement doughnut. Chocolate was required to fortify me against jet lag induced exhaustion.

The scent of fish and chips draw me into a pub. It's all polished wood and brass, sticky floors and laughter echoing off the walls for at least the last few hundred years.

I sling my bags onto one side of a small booth and take a seat under a frosted green lamp. I study the menu, just to read, to focus, and to give the rest of my thoughts a chance to pause.

"Hello. Can I take your order?" asks a cheery woman with graying hair.

"Fish and chips. Thanks." Without the menu to keep me occupied, I take out the map Antonio gave me and spread it on the wooden table. There were a handful of places Marcus and I wanted to visit in London. I have a few days before Paris or was it Amsterdam first? I'll have to check the itinerary Hazel made. I text Jesse again, feeling a twinge of anxiety. Exhausted, I blink rapidly a few times. The wooden bench of the booth starts to look like an inviting place to take a nap.

When the food comes, starved, I don't bother folding up the map, using it as a placemat for the greasy meal. I power down the fish and chips, drizzled with vinegar, but my stomach wants more.

Guests fill the room, fixated on the TV airing a soccer game. A couple at the neighboring table gets up to leave. The wife complains about the fried food, stating she can't stand to eat another basket of fries.

I eye them, untouched along with a little tub of dipping sauce that I didn't get with my order. It wouldn't do any harm to snag them, right?

I swish my lips from side to side, debating. I must be really tired. Nonetheless, I casually stand over the table as if I'm looking for a spare napkin and then swipe the basket of fries and scoot back over to my booth.

They're cold but I don't care. It's food and I'm still hungry. And tired. Have I mentioned that?

And don't get all grossed out. You know you've spotted uneaten food or a tray in the hall of a hotel and entertained it. No sense in letting perfectly good, untouched French fries go to waste.

As I stuff another "chip," as they're called here, in my mouth, the busboy clears the other table. Then his hand brushes mine as I reach for my glass.

"Excuse me," he says in accented English though it sounds more like *scusa.*

We both freeze, gripping the glass.

Our eyes meet.

Mine narrow.

Before the words, *What are you doing here?* come out of my mouth, my server lets out a cheerful laugh. "Antonio is always right on it, making sure we don't run out of dishes. We did, on his first day." She lowers her voice to a whisper. "The dishwasher broke, but we didn't tell him that. Keeps him on his toes. He's probably been the longest surviving busboy though I'd hardly call him a boy."

I get the sense she doesn't think he can understand her.

His lips quirk and he winks, but he doesn't verbally acknowledge me. Um, hello, Romeo. We met. Twice.

Maybe he's a look alike, fresh off the handsome Italian male assembly line?

Perhaps I dozed off and this is a dream. I pinch myself discretely beneath the table. Nope. Awake and as tired as ever.

Busy, he deposits a bucket of empty plates and bowls in a cart and moves on to the nearby vacant table.

The server sits across from me and goes on, "I don't mind if he sticks around." She waggles her brows. "For a while, it was like we got a new busboy each week. I, on the other hand, have been here so long sometimes I forget I'm at work. Here I am, thinking it's my dining room and I can just sit down whenever I want. But where are my proper British manners? I'm Justine by the way." She doesn't bother getting up.

I like her. Justine and I could be buddies. We could both nap, giving a new meaning to a restaurant booth. Bunk booths. Booth buddies.

I introduce myself and we chat a while before she takes an order to another table.

She didn't leave me a bill, and not knowing the protocol in England, I wait and then watch if guests pay at the podium by the front. Other servers leave the bill with their tables and I wonder if Justine forgot, but she doesn't stop long enough for me to get her attention.

I take out a wad of bills and leave them on the table, gather up my stuff, and exit.

Outside, when I push through a clog of tourists gathered around a red umbrella, even though it's not raining, the busboy calls, "*Scusa, bella.*"

Recognizing the voice, I stagger back, knocking into someone with my bag. "Sorry," I say, feeling dizzy and disoriented.

Antonio stuffs the money into my hand, shaking his head. "Justine wants you to keep it."

"Huh?" I don't fully understand anything other than the fact that Antonio smells like expensive cologne and comfort—at odds with his busboy status and yet perfectly fitting. Must be an Italian guy thing. They come prepackaged smelling delicious.

His eyes, with golden flecks around the edges, hypnotize me for a moment. He repeats, "No payment," breaking the spell. "Get yourself dessert. There's a great gelato cart in the Red Market."

Then I realize Justine must've seen me bedraggled with all my bags and stealing the fries off someone else's table, thinking I'm a hobo. What can I say? Food waste is wrong. I open my mouth to explain that I'm not a drifter, but Antonio is gone in a flurry of busboy black, sun-kissed skin, and loose, tousled dark brown curls.

I shout, "Thank you," but I don't think he hears me over the blare of a cab and the striking of Big Ben's bell for the quarter-hour.

I tuck the cash away and continue, strolling along the Thames past notable buildings. My tally of classic red telephone boxes is eight. Tour buses line the road to my left and belch diesel exhaust. I'm thankful for the shade of the overhanging trees and the damp basement breeze off the river.

For the first time, I'm glad to be here. But as I continue along the ribbon of water, adjusting my bag, the heft reminds me of how much baggage I carry. And I can't help wonder if I'll be able to leave any of it behind.

CHAPTER 4
A KISS BY ANY OTHER NAME
ANTONIO

There's a saying in English, I think it's *Third time is Charming*. Or the charm? Something like that. Seeing Colette three times in one day in a city as big as this feels like luck, like serendipity.

Or a mega reminder to stay away from American women. I know better than to flirt with disaster or love—not that I expect to find the true, everlasting kind anyway.

The words to ask her if she'd like to get together later were on my tongue but got tangled up in translation...or maybe it was my brain trying to protect me. We have an intense moment of back and forth quibbling.

Me: Oh, come on. She's cute yet sassy, in an All-American kind of way.

Brain: That's what you said last time.

Me: I was young and foolish.

Brain: You still are.

Me: That's rude. I've grown, matured.

My brain doesn't deny my accusation but silently ignores me.

Instead of asking Colette to meet me for coffee later or something, I hurried back inside because I'd just barely gotten my job back after being gone longer than I'd meant when I'd traveled to

Glasgow—busboys must be in short supply or maybe Justine has an affinity for me.

And perhaps my brain has a point. I've made more than a few mistakes with women since that first brush with love. I've been called charming, a scoundrel, a tease, and a few unkind words in French, Italian, and Spanish that I won't repeat.

After my shift bussing tables, I pass Victoria Embankment, Blackfriars, and continue walking until I spot London Bridge. A crowd of tourists bustling by me on the sidewalk force me into the street. A car horn blares as it swipes past.

I shout a few unkind words in Italian...and French and Spanish just to cover my bases.

Finding a bench, I pull out the journal. I skim the London entries for the tenth...millionth time. I'm waiting for a clue, something to jump out at me. Still nothing.

One of my mother's favorite places was Tower Bridge. It's not far and I've already been there a half dozen times, but if I can piece together the places she's been, maybe they'll lead me to her.

Cheering and laughter echo across the river. A boat, pulling a giant yellow rubber duck cruises through the water. I only just realize there's a man seated on the other end of the bench. He smells like dirty laundry. Or maybe it's me from my shift at the pub.

"Not something you see every day." His accent isn't British or American English, Australian perhaps. One of his hands rests on a cart, the kind old-world grandmothers tote behind them on their trips to the market. A tattered, black plastic bag lines his. There's a folded piece of cardboard and lots of other plastic bags stuffed inside. He laughs and shakes his head as the enormous duck draws closer, glowing brightly in the pale sapphire twilight.

The two of us sit there, watching as the duck passes. The people in the tugboat wave at the crowd gathered along the edge of the river. I watch them: mothers and fathers, sons and daughters, grandparents, friends, and tourists. Could she be out there? She could be anywhere. My emotions snake through me, up and down, high and low.

When the duck has passed, the sun lowers behind the bridge, winking goodnight among the gathering clouds.

The homeless guy grunts and mumbles, "Another day." Then he says, "Still haven't found what I'm looking for."

"Me neither," I mumble.

Then he hums a bar of a familiar song and I realize those were lyrics, not a comment to me.

What am I looking for? My mother. A connection to my past to help me figure out who I am because I refuse to be bound by my father. He's a monster. And I can only imagine she left because of that. But she left me with him.

When I think harder about that, the real reason I'm looking for her is to ask *why*. Why'd she abandon me?

I get up and the man reclines on the bench.

As the night closes in around me and shutters my thoughts for now. Mist glows around the overhead street lights. The eerie sound of the water lapping against the ancient brick walls makes me shiver. I can't pull the dark close like a blanket and that's what I need, a blanket and a bed, but I force myself forward until I reach London Bridge.

Before I get there, the clouds break. Rain pours down. Typical London. I take cover under the overhang of a building, but a steady drip, drip, drip runs down my back from somewhere above. I check my phone. It's getting late. That walk took longer than I remember. The Tube will stop running soon.

I should just give up, but press on, propelled by foolish hope. I worry that the one time I turn back will be the time she'll be right around the bend. I pass a closed bookseller and a graffitied undercroft. Lights flood it to deter vandals.

As the rain continues to pour down, I dash under to keep dry. Someone else huddles beneath it, shivering.

A strand of blond hair peeks out from under a hood. "Colette?" I ask, hardly believing my eyes.

She startles and then there's a whistle. Once more, I help her to her feet, gripping both her arms.

Movement from farther down the wall catches my eye as a figure, surrounded by painted swirls and streaks of red and blue and black, gathers up a backpack and scurries away.

"Are you okay?" I ask her.

Before she answers, a police officer rushes toward us from the opposite direction, whistling and wielding a club. "I thought flooding this place with light would keep you hooligans away. Doing a rotten job playing lookout, huh?"

Worried he's going to haul us off, I shake my head and then lean toward Colette. Without thinking, I frame her face with my hands and kiss her passionately on the lips to make the cop think we're a couple trying to keep dry and warm. I'd rather not have another altercation with an officer of the law.

The cop grouses. "Oh, I see what you're up to. Move along." He shakes the club at us.

Colette's eyes are as wide as coins, her face pale and popping with freckles, and her lips stung pink like raspberries.

Gripping her by the arm, I hurry us back into the rain. We race along the sidewalk until a shop with an awning comes into view.

When we stop underneath, she exclaims, "What was that?"

"What was what?"

She sputters as droplets of water run down her face and drip from her chin. She sparkles in the dim light.

"You—" Her eyes widen more. "You kissed me."

"Yeah, because the cop would've taken our information if he thought we were connected to that hooligan, as he called him."

"What hooligan?"

"The one who spray-painted the wall next to you."

She sinks back. "Oh. I must've fallen asleep. Rule number three-hundred ten..." She trails off.

"You're lucky the vandal didn't rob you."

Frantic, she rummages through her bags, checking. "Did he rob me?"

"First of all, sleeping in public places is prohibited. Second of all, it's dangerous. Third of all—"

She pumps her palms in the air. "I get it. I get it. I must've fallen asleep. I didn't mean to." She wipes her hand down her face. "Jet lag." A slim gold ring on her fourth finger catches in the light.

"I'm sorry," I say abruptly. "I didn't know."

"Didn't know that I have jet lag?" she asks.

"No, that you're married. I would never have—" I may be a Romeo, as she'd said when we first met, but I have a strict rule about only involving myself with single women. Not that the kiss meant anything.

Though her lips were especially soft. Warm, despite the cold rain. Welcoming even though she clearly wants nothing to do with me.

Confusion folds her features. "I'm not married."

Both my eyebrows shoot up and I gaze at the ring.

Her fingers touch it. "Oh. This. I was married." She looks into the falling rain as if to quell sadness.

"We should get you somewhere warm. Dry. Where are you staying?"

"I was supposed to meet my friend's childhood friend Jesse. We'd arranged to meet by the bridge. But she never showed up. Maybe because of the rain. That's when I doubled back to find someplace dry."

"You're welcome to come back to my place."

She cocks her head. "Nice try, but I'll get a hotel. And, uh, thanks for helping me out back there, being my decoy. Fell off the turnip truck, again."

"That was a close scrape. In the future, I recommend avoiding shady places under bridges."

"Noted. You never know who might just try to maul you with his mouth." I can't tell if she's joking.

"Are you saying I'm a bad kisser? I've never gotten a poor review," I say with laughter in my voice.

She balks. "Well, aren't you Mr. Confident? I meant that it was surprising."

"So was finding you huddled under a bridge. At least let me get you something warm to drink. Then I'll walk you to a hotel. You shouldn't wander the streets alone."

"I'm wandering with a purpose, on a whimsy as my friend Minnie calls it," she says through a shiver.

I fight the urge to wrap my arm around her. Although she claims not to be married, I don't want to overstep her bounds.

"So no husband. Do you have a boyfriend?"

Her eyebrows knit together. "You sure are nosy for having just met me."

"This is our fourth meeting."

"So are you saying that it's okay that we kissed since it wasn't our first date?"

"A date?" My laughter bounces off the stone buildings as we walk.

She slows. "What's so funny?"

"Colette, if I took you on a date, you'd know it." I don't mean it arrogantly, but I make sure the women I date have a good time.

"I just meant that as...never mind."

A long pause stretches between us as we near one of my favorite booksellers.

She pauses under the overhang and gazes at an illuminated copy of Shakespeare's *A Midsummer's Night Dream.*

I step behind her and recite a few lines. She turns slowly to face me and picks up where I left off.

For the briefest of moments, our gazes connect.

"People always comment on the color of another person's eyes. But that's not the whole story. In yours, I see sadness, wonder...beauty. They reflect the way you see the world. Right now, I see an adventure."

"And I see another police officer approaching," she says abruptly, craning her head around me.

My lips quirk flirtatiously. "Should I kiss you again?"

Instead, she grips my arm and we run, splashing through the puddles in the streets.

"Is this what wandering with a purpose is?" I ask when we slow down.

That, at last, wins me a smile. It magnetizes me despite my better sensibilities.

Across the street, a small group pours out of a pub. "Shall we?" I ask.

"Shall we what?" she asks.

"Go on an adventure. What is it they say in America? I have people to do, places to go, and things to see."

She winces. "Not quite."

"Let me get you something to warm you up." I point to the pub.

"I should find a place to stay before I fall asleep again. Raincheck?" she asks.

I hold my hand up. "It is raining."

She tips her head back and laughs. "That's another saying. Meaning, I'd like to take you up on your offer another time."

"So you're agreeing to go on a date with me?"

"I didn't say that. And you didn't ask me." She places her hand on her hip at a sassy angle.

"Touché."

"Ah, so you do know some American sayings."

Wearing a smirk, I tap the air with my finger. "I think that one is French."

"Touché," she repeats.

This would be a moment to laugh together, but she holds back, leaving me wanting more.

CHAPTER 5
SASSY AND SOUTHERN
COLETTE

Last night, in a haze, I hardly paid attention to the hotel Antonio walked me to. I only vaguely remember checking in. But I do recall his lips on mine when he woke me from the strangest dream—shame on me for falling asleep under a bridge like an idiot. Under a bridge! I give new meaning to green travel.

But the kiss. The way his lips fit around mine. The soft urgency. The gentle demand. The way it made my legs like noodles. My brain like butter.

I must be hungry.

But there was no denying passion filled that brief kiss in the rain. Well, more like under a bridge kind of, but there was something romantic about it.

About Antonio.

That dark, tousled hair.

The tasteful stubble.

The light dimple in his chin.

His eyes rimmed gold.

The roughness in voice.

Never mind. He's a Romeo—a heartbreaker—if there ever

was one. I'm not looking for that kind of adventure. The one that would leave me lonely and longing.

As I fully wake, I take in the crown molding on the hotel room ceiling, the gold frame around an oil painting, and the Princess and the Pea bed.

I sit up and stretch. The heavy, gilt drapes are parted slightly, letting in a stream of sunlight. The antique clock across the room shows that it's late afternoon.

"Oops." I did not mean to sleep that long. I blame jet lag.

Never mind falling off the turnip truck yesterday, I drove that thing into the River Thames. What was I thinking? I get to my feet, looking around the luxurious room. "This is more like it."

After taking a long shower, I text Hazel. So much for her friend Jesse.

I don't tell her about my many mishaps: nearly falling off the edge of a fountain in the name of doing it for the 'Gram, eating a double serving of French fries, passing out in the rain, or meeting Antonio.

Nope, she'd just get worried. Well, not about the last part. She'd encourage me.

Hazel replies with a lot of apologetic emojis.

Hazel: So sorry. Jesse got hung up yesterday. Just wait. You'll have so much fun.

Me: I'd been waiting...for hours by the bridge until it started raining.

She makes more apologies and then arranges for Jesse and me to meet at a teashop. I ask for her friend's number but Hazel doesn't answer.

I can only imagine this hotel costs a fortune. I'm by no means traveling on a backpacker's budget like I would have done with Marcus, but I'll have to find the original hotel Hazel and Maxwell booked for me. This place with its Elizabethan décor, statues, and fancy furniture likely isn't included on the travel points plan.

I stop short of reenacting a bouncing-on-the-bed scene like in the movies.

When I head downstairs to check out, amidst what looks like foreign dignitaries in their finery, I stick out like a sore foot—from all that walking yesterday. I definitely don't fit in, wearing a denim skirt and tank top. Hazel packed for me in under an hour and didn't plan on tea with London's aristocracy. This is no Holiday Inn.

At the main desk, I pass my key to the concierge. "Hi, I'd like to check out."

He types on a computer and then gives me a slight nod.

Confused, I ask, "Um, how much is it?"

"All paid up, miss."

"Yes, but the cost?"

He barely conceals his sigh of annoyance and presents me with a bill.

My gaze jerks to the price. It's one of those *if you have to ask, you can't afford it* situations. Then I see the name next to the credit card information. *Antonio Moretti.*

I tuck my chin. "He paid for it?" I snap my fingers. "I knew he was no stranger to designer labels. Thanks to Hazel, I notice things like that."

The concierge's lips purse like my grandmama's used to if her fuse was running short.

"May I help you with anything else, miss?"

"I'm from the south. I know that's just a polite way of telling me to get lost. Thank you, sir. I shall be on my way."

As I exit into the gray light of the afternoon, Antonio's words from the night before filter back. "*Shall we*?"

Shall we go on an adventure? A date?

"Get that handsome heartthrob out of your head, Colette," I mutter.

The doorman gives me a cross-eyed look.

I get the sense I don't quite belong in this part of town, so I start walking. After a while, I try to orient myself.

Park. Building. Other building.

Oh, I'm lost alright.

It's nearly four and I'm supposed to meet Jesse. Rather, I wanted to visit Buckingham Palace today. Also, on the bucket list is the Globe Theater and the London Eye.

This is supposed to be a summer to remember. Maybe a way to create closure on the past—more like getting distracted by a handsome Italian. And thrown off by rainy weather. I resolve to focus and keep my arms and legs inside the turnip truck.

At least Hazel arranged for me to meet Jesse at a teashop. I'm starved.

When I arrive, I look around for someone Hazel would be friends with—tall, elegant, European.

A couple talks intimately by the window. Three women chat animatedly, making me miss my besties. And no less than four people type intently on their laptops.

No Jesse. Figures.

I get myself a tea and two scones. Remember, no judgment. The blueberry looked scrummy, as they say here, and I need something with chocolate. Priorities, people.

Finding a vacant table, I sit down.

Before my tea is cool enough to drink, a scruffy guy stands behind the chair opposite me. "Colette?" he asks then points to himself. "Jesse." He wears a dark blue T-shirt, black jeans, and a buzzcut. Lips on the thin side hover around a foxlike smile.

Tall? Yes.

Elegant? No.

"I missed you yesterday. I got wrapped up in—" He leaves off vaguely as he turns the chair around backward and plonks down.

"You're not a female. Hazel is going to hear it from me."

He smirks. "No. Definitely not. But you're welcome to stay with me." Now, his smirk borders on criminal.

I straighten in my chair. "No problem. I found a place to stay."

"Where's that?"

"Four Seasons," I blurt, omitting that it was just one night.

He nods as if impressed. "Fancy. I was in that neighborhood last night like you, Princess."

"Yeah. You were supposed to meet me at Tower Bridge."

He gazes at his pale, slender fingers. Gray, black, and blue ink tints the tips and nailbeds. "Yeah. Waited around. Didn't see you. Started to rain."

A deep V forms between my brows. "I think I saw you. Were you spray—?" Forget Antonio being my decoy. We were this hooligan's distraction so he could make a get away.

Jesse's laughter fills the room. "I was being free! Making the world a more beautiful place." He downs my tea and gets to his feet.

My mouth falls open as I stare at my empty cup.

"Come with me. Hazel told me to show you the beautiful parts of London."

I'm not so sure our definitions of beautiful are in sync. "I'm not going anywhere until you get me another cup of tea."

"Free refills." He lopes away with the cup in hand.

"In a clean cup," I call not wanting any of his icky germs.

I drop my face into my hands. This trip is going wrong. So wrong. I knew it was a bad idea.

When Jesse gets back, I say, "First, I thought you were a girl."

"Definitely not. But you are." His laugh is husky. "Why? Do you have to call your boyfriend?" he challenges boldly.

My eyebrows knit together. "No, I don't have a boyfriend." I kick myself under the table. I should've said yes. Antonio. The trinket seller by Whitehall. Anyone.

This guy eyes my scone hungrily. Then me.

I squirm.

"Good. Then I have you all to myself." He takes a big bite.

I grip my phone, ready to text Hazel in ALL CAPS, but the battery died. I pull out my charger and then eye the plug next to the table. Great. Wrong kind. "Didn't consider the conversion. I need to charge my phone. Can you help me with that?" I ask not knowing the first thing about European electricity.

The corner of Jesse's lip lifts and he nods. "Of course. I can do anything."

"I don't even want to know what you mean by that," I mutter.

"You need an adapter. Can I see your phone?" he asks.

I place it on the table between us and he takes it in his paint-speckled hands.

"Don't move." In one deft, sticky-fingered movement, Jesse makes off with my phone.

I get to my feet and open my mouth to call after him, but he's gone, with my phone. With my phone!

I scramble, gather my things and rush outside, but he's not on the street. I go back inside, not sure what to do. Report him? Go to the U.S. Embassy?

Rule number something or other, *when separated from your party, stay put until they find you*. My party is my phone so I'll stay here. Maybe Jesse will come back…and Marcus too. Wishful thinking.

At the table, my scone remains on the table so I stress-stuff it in my mouth.

He's coming right back. I repeat this like a mantra.

However, Jesse's backpack sits on the chair opposite me. Likely, it contains illegal contraband. I toe it with my foot. Should probably call in a bomb squad. You never know.

My leg jiggles. I sip the coffee and nibble half of the other scone he touched with his lying lips.

The clock on the wall shaped like a coffee bean tells me nearly an hour has passed.

He's not coming back.

Where's Antonio when you need him?

I pull out the fish and chips grease-stained map he gave me yesterday. I guess I'm doing this analog...and I'll find that police officer and report Jesse.

The chair opposite me scrapes against the floor and I startle from my thoughts. Jesse holds out a converter and my phone. "Found it," he repeats and guzzles his now-cold coffee.

"Thank you." Surprised, I plug the wire into the socket on the wall below the table.

"See, I'm a useful person to know, Princess." Jesse tips back in the chair, folding his hands behind his head.

I squint, not sure what to make of this semi-sketchy guy. A rogue knight to my damsel in distress? That's not the role I want to play, but I haven't exactly hit the ground running since arriving here in London.

"What kind of person are you?" he asks.

"I'm not a princess," I answer and I'm not breaking my rules for solo travel again. I will stay aboard the turnip truck.

Jesse stretches his arms wide as he rules this kingdom. "Jesse the rebel. Jesse the wild. Jesse the free."

I think I'm in a fever dream. Caught my death out there in the rain last night.

His words drip with daring. "Hazel said you have a bucket list. I've always wanted to be a tourist. Come on. Let's go. Seize the day and all that. No time like the present whatever, whatever. Fortune favors the bold etcetera, etcetera."

This idiot savant drags me by the wrist out of the coffee shop and toward a woman wearing a scarf tied neatly around her neck, leading a group of tourists wearing T-shirts and baseball hats, chattering in American English. We move en masse toward a double-decker bus.

Jesse whispers, "Just stick with me."

He leads me up the impossibly narrow and steep stairs to the top and then to the back.

"Did you plan for this? Pay for—?" My heart races with anxiety as I jerk loose from his hold.

Jesse holds one finger over my lips. "Shh. We're a young couple, on our honeymoon in Europe. I'm Robert and you're… Hmm." He studies me. "You're Anna. We met at university, fell madly in love, and have a cat named Poppy. I've always wanted a kitten." Jesse? Robert? Weirdo? Whoever this guy is wears a roguish grin. Pulling out a permanent marker, he writes on the back of the seat. *Property of Robert and Anna.*

I have never been party to illegal activities, except on senior day back in high school—and the popcorn thing—, but that was a prank-level prohibition, not criminal activity.

My mouth hangs open. I goggle in disbelief that he wrote on the seat. I fear he's one trigger-happy finger away from busting out the spray paint.

He pinches my chin and leans close, whispering, "I'm going to take you to the palace."

"Buckingham Palace?" I tuck away, wresting myself from his grasp again.

"No, you're coming home with me. You can meet the whole family. But first, there's more adventure to be had."

I preferred the Antonio style of adventure—or the stay-at-home kind. Is this guy for real? Never mind the turnip truck. He's on the wacky wagon. And I want to get off. Now.

The bus crawls down Regent Street, nearing Piccadilly Circus.

I spot the fountain where I first met Antonio.

And there, like a beacon, like an actual knight in shining armor, he stands with a camera in hand, snapping a photo of the statue of the Greek god Eros.

I cup my hands around my mouth and shout his name. "Romeo, Romeo! I mean, Antonio. Help me!"

Dressed in dark blue jeans and a black shirt, he turns, scanning his surroundings.

I wave wildly.

Jesse looks at me. "You like Shakespeare?"

"I'm no Juliet, buddy," I say, elbowing past him as the bus creeps forward.

He grabs my arm. "Where do you think you're going?"

I'm a good southern girl at heart, but my gift is not in being reserved—the last twenty-four hours notwithstanding. In fact, my mother called me *The Mouth*. As in, *That girl has a sassy mouth on her. That girl can't keep her mouth shut. That girl...*

Am I still that girl?

Jesse's expression darkens.

I grit my teeth and grind out, "Let me go."

"And if I don't want to?" That roguish grin of his returns.

"You'll find out what a girl like me can do with popcorn, duct tape, and a whole lotta sass."

I turn, ready to make a grand exit (erm, ghost-like exit because I don't want to get in trouble in a foreign country) when Antonio vaults over the side of the bus. His muscles tense. His gaze darkens.

Everyone gasps.

Jesse staggers back as the bus lurches but quickly regains his footing.

Forget about passing out under the bridge, kissing Antonio in the rain, and boarding the bus without a ticket, I'm in trouble now.

CHAPTER 6
PRINCESS CHARMING
ANTONIO

Call me a hopeless romantic, but after yesterday's chance encounters with Colette, I couldn't get her out of my head.

We didn't exchange numbers. I don't even know her. However, I returned to Piccadilly to capture what I could the memory of our first meeting…and get another doughnut. It's breakfast time somewhere.

Spotting her on the top of the red double-decker bus, I cast one quick look at Eros and am certain this has nothing to do with coincidence.

For a moment, I feel like Romeo to her Juliet, but the strain in her voice as she calls my name and the skinny guy gripping her arm tells me otherwise. As she tries to shrug him off, the tough Italian my father raised takes over. I dodge cars as I rush through traffic, grip the ladder on the side of the bus, and land up top on my feet.

"Colette? Are you okay?" I stride forward as the bus passes Trafalgar Square and the park I visited yesterday.

The other guy's lips peel back in a leer. "Romeo? She just said she's not Juliet, so I'll just send you back the way you came." The sharpness in his eyes and the way his fists coil at his sides tell me he's no stranger to fighting.

Then again, neither am I with no thanks to my father. "Is he bothering you?" I ask Colette.

"I just want to get off this bus." She wrings her hands, confused, stricken, and relieved all at once.

We wheeze past the stately Buckingham Palace before coming to a stop.

The driver appears with a tour guide. "Excuse me. Several passengers reported a problem up here. May I see your passes?"

"Thanks, but there's no problem," I say. "We're just getting off."

I clasp Colette's hand in mine and we stride past.

The guy with the low brow that was hassling her follows us, bellowing, "Oh, there's a problem, alright."

Once on the sidewalk, I move to hurry us away—better not to engage with a guy like this.

Colette stops abruptly. "Jesse, the only problem is that you mistook me for someone named Anna. Nope. Colette Clark will not be messed with. Thanks for sharing your phone charger," she says, tossing a wire to him.

He wears a cocky smile. "I'm not good at sharing or asking. I lifted that from a shop."

"You stole it?" she asks, aghast.

"I did it for you, but you did steal my interest. I like you. You could be useful." His nose is crooked like it's been broken.

My jaw ticks and I move closer, but Colette grips my arm.

Jesse continues, "Anything for you, Princess. Fitting that we're outside the palace. Lots of sparkly things in there. Lucky for us, I know a secret way in. Come on, let's go have some fun."

I sense that he's a low-level, petty criminal, which is nothing compared to my family. Not that I condone any of that kind of activity.

Colette huffs. "Our definition of fun is wildly different. We'll pay for our tickets, thank you very much."

He abruptly moves toward her.

I step in front protectively. "You're going to turn around, walk away, and forget all about your nasty little fantasy," I grind out.

He levels his gaze at me. "What are you going to do about it? If you haven't noticed, these are my streets."

Two surly guys with menacing stances stalk toward us. He must've called in backup.

"Where are my manners? I'm Antonio Moretti," I emphasize the last name. If he's into thievery, he'll recognize the meaning behind it. "What do you call yourself?" If I'm right about him, he's all fire and flame. He's a fuse, fuel, and explosive. He'll blow but then burn out. I've seen it before. He thinks he's tough, but I know all about guys like him.

"Trying to edge in on my territory?" Jesse counters.

"Your territory?" I chuckle. "The only reason you're getting away with any of this is because Ro lets you."

Jesse glares. "I'm talking about the girl."

"She's not property."

"If you're in the business, with a pretty face like that you must recognize that she could be very useful."

"And *she* is standing right here," Colette says, her gaze catting from Jesse to me. "I suggest you boys take your little hen fight somewhere else."

"So she's with you?" Jesse asks.

"I'm not with anyone. And cluck, cluck." At that, she juts her elbows and flaps them twice like a chicken before turning away.

I don't know whether to chuckle or recognize a new menace on these streets. I appreciate that Colette is standing up for herself, but cannot fathom how she ended up with this thug. My attention follows her and in that split second turning my back, Jesse lunges for me.

I shove him off, rapid-fire Italian spewing out of my mouth. I stalk forward, fists ready to pound.

The other two guys take off, realizing I wasn't joking about the family name. It's not something I'm proud of, but I'm all too familiar with lowlifes like them. A top-tier name is the only threat they'll respond to as evidenced by the scabs and scars they bear. Neither aggression nor arrest deters them from causing trouble.

Why Jesse got it in his head that Colette belongs to him is beyond me. Where'd she meet this loser?

A few people stop to gawk. I don't want to be filmed by tourists all too pleased to report they saw a real-life street fight while on holiday. The attention is definitely something I want to avoid as well.

"I suggest you forget about Colette," I hiss.

"But she's a princess. No one could forget about her."

He's not wrong.

Who is this American girl who's possessed us? No. Scratch that. I know better than to get tangled up with women like her. I just want to make sure she's safe. It's one thing to go sightseeing in a foreign country. It's another to fall asleep under a bridge and somehow fall in with London's underbelly.

I step closer, towering over Jesse. "Move along."

"Alright, alright, Moretti. I'll forget about her, but I won't forget about you. We'll be seeing each other again, I'm sure." A threat hides in the offhand comment.

Colette nears the corner, and I'm afraid to let her out of my sight.

I lean into Jesse so no one else can hear. "If we do, mine will be the last face you see."

I'd never do the kinds of things my father and his guys pull off, but I'll let Jesse think what he will.

Adrenaline and anger pulse through me as Jesse stalks away. I hurry after Colette to find her around the corner, leaning against a brick wall and shaking.

I grip her upper arms. "Are you okay?"

She looks at the ground. "This is a mess. I'm sorry."

"Do I want to know where you found that guy?"

She swipes her hand across her forehead. "You must think I'm a hapless, clueless, country bumpkin."

"No, I think you took a wrong turn somewhere."

She paces like the palace guards and pulls out her phone. "This thing won't hold its charge, but when I can, I'm going to call Hazel and give her a piece of my mind. That guy was insane. Dangerous. Drunk? He had to have had a couple of pints with his breakfast. A screw loose. An egg short a dozen." She recounts how they ended up on the double-decker bus.

"I don't think he'll bother you again."

Her eyes widen. "And you just come out of nowhere, scale the side of a bus, and—"

The question she edges toward is not something I want to explain.

She eyes the castle. "I'd like to hide under a blanket or inside that guard booth. Although the bed last night would be preferable. By the way, you did not have to pay for my hotel room."

"You were practically asleep on your feet. I wanted to make sure you got a good night's rest and didn't get into any more trouble. Clearly, I fell short."

"I guess it keeps finding me. But thank you. I owe you. Twice now."

I tip my head from side to side. "I accept most forms of payment."

"Ha ha. At least let me buy you a ticket to the palace. Have you been?"

Several times, but I keep that to myself so we can spend a bit more time together.

The sky threatens to rain as we cross to Buckingham Palace and leave the altercation on the sidewalk. Twilight falls as we tour the gilded rooms, laced with history. My mother's entry in the journal comes to mind. She'd walk these same halls, imagining herself a princess.

Colette isn't a princess after all. No, her crown is bigger, brighter. She's beautiful. Royalty with those big, brown eyes, her long silky hair, and curves that make me think of a sunny afternoon in Tuscany. When the docent announces it's nearly closing time, we peer into the rain by the exit.

Colette puffs a long exhale. "I need to get an umbrella."

"You and me both. I still can't get used to the rain."

"You're from Italy, right?"

"The south. Mediterranean climate. Rain is relatively rare."

"Must be nice."

"Unless your last name is Moretti. Then there are obligations. Expectations. My mother was from London. Kristy Nichols. Met my father on holiday. She liked this kind of thing though." I gesture around us, but change subjects. "Where's your hotel reservation?"

Colette shows me a website on her phone. "After the close encounter with Jesse, I'm not sure I should trust Hazel's recommendations."

"It's not the Four Seasons, but I've been by there. Looks clean. Safe." That's what I want. To keep her safe. The only way my mother could be safe was to leave. Same with me. Then again, I know my father will eventually find me. But will I find her?

Colette sighs as if this trip is a total failure. Like my mother's memories of London, I want her to have something good to write home about. For now, I'll indulge this fantasy with her.

"Do you want something to eat?"

"Like a date?" Her throat bobs with what seems like uncertainty, perhaps at my earlier comment.

I try to suppress a smile. "Not what I had in mind. Just a warm meal." My brain is adamant this time. Nope. Not getting involved. Colette is trouble. Finds trouble. Would cause me trouble.

"Jesse doesn't know where you live, does he?" she asks.

"No. And he doesn't seem like the kind of guy who'd *extract* revenge. At least not on me."

"You mean exact revenge?"

Half the time, I make these mistakes just to see her smile.

"Well, if he shows up again, maybe my sassy southern mouth can talk us out of trouble."

"I'd wager on it and your charm."

She squawks a laugh. "Me? Charming? No, you've got the wrong princess. But dinner would be nice. I'm so hungry I could eat a scabby raccoon."

I wrinkle my nose.

"See? Not charming."

Laughter is on my lips. Help me, please. "The charmingest."

She pokes me again, in the side this time. Her touch is like a wand, sending magic flowing through me. "We have to work on your English."

"Okay, professor. And we'll take the scenic route to stay out of the rain."

We wind along endless streets, some sooty, others perfumed. We pass through clouds of curry and the day's news with headlines I ignore. A covered market sells everything from flowers to fish to felt. The cobbled streets narrow, but they're tidy with spindly trees lining the sidewalk.

I point to a lane up ahead. "We're almost there."

I pat my pockets and tip my head toward the sky as it pours. "Not good. I forgot my key."

"Do you have one hidden somewhere? Or we could just go to a restaurant."

"I may work as a busboy, but I can cook." I wink. "Come on, it'll be worth it."

We slip down an alleyway and reach a large metal gate at the end. "Can you climb?" I ask, folding my hands together for her to step on.

She hesitates. "Can I see your license and registration, sir?"

I get the joke from an American movie I saw. "I promise, I am not part of a crime ring or going to suggest we rob the joint. This is my place. I pay my rent in full every month."

"And you forgot your keys?" She uses air-quotes.

"I do at least twice a week. Usually, I call the owner, but she's out of town this weekend." And she's ready to have my head on a platter for having to let me in so often. Back home, locks on doors only kept honest people out and my father doesn't run with too many of those kinds of folks.

"Okay. Can't be worse than waking up under a bridge. Jesse was the hooligan with the spray paint by the way. He arranged to meet me by the bridge all right. Guess he got distracted." She hoists herself up.

I was the one who got distracted by her lips. Much like I do now, but I force myself to focus as I scale the fence.

On the other side, we pass through the garden entryway, though the flowers in the pots wither in the summer heat and the path needs sweeping. I check under the mat.

"Must've forgotten to replace the key." I try the door, but it doesn't budge. "I'm lousy at remembering stuff like this."

"You mean adulting? Keeping track of important things like your key?"

I ignore the teasing dig and run my hand through my hair then glance up at an open window. "You'll have to go through and let me in."

"Sounds like breaking and entering."

"I promise I won't call the cops."

"At this point, I might be better off in jail." Colette sighs and braces my shoulders, preparing for me to give her another boost.

CHAPTER 7
BREAKING, ENTERING & EATING
COLETTE

We're just not going to think too hard about how I got myself into this situation.

Are you wondering which situation? Not the one where I fell asleep under a bridge. I know, I know. Dumb. I'm aware.

Not the one where I practically went on a crime spree with a British bad boy. Hazel is going to hear it from me about her beloved childhood best friend. Jesse? Not Jessy or Jessie. She could've at least warned me it was a dude. Oh. Now I get her angle. She was trying to make a love connection.

I have standards, thank you very much.

And not the situation when the aforementioned thug backed down when Antonio did some name dropping. Of his own name. What was that about? I have no idea. Figuring out things like that is what tomorrow is for.

Okay? Okay.

The current situation is the one where I tipped top over teakettle through a narrow window and into someone's bathroom. At least the marble is nice...and clean. But whose house is this? Antonio's? I don't know what to believe.

But the real problem here is my skirt rode up as I shot

through the window opening, revealing what they call *knickers* here in England.

Yes, while I slithered through the window, my underwear was on full display for the world to see. Well, Antonio. Though it may as well be the world.

According to my mother, God bless her, there are three underwear classifications. There are the *pretty panties* with fancy little frills. There are *period panties*, which are self-explanatory. Then there are *practical panties*. Sometimes they're plain, simple, perhaps have a full seat. My particular pair have a rainbow pattern...and a unicorn on the butt. Yup.

Maybe I'll just stay in here for a day or two or ten. Antonio will get tired of waiting outside and hit the road.

What's more embarrassing than finding out that a thug stole you a phone charger?

Having a stranger glimpse your unmentionables. Well, Antonio isn't quite a stranger. We've kissed, but you know what I mean.

"You get in okay?" Antonio hollers up in his charming accent.

"Yup. Fine. Just getting situated. Oriented. Combobulated." I'll stop rambling now.

"I don't know that last word."

"It's the opposite of discombobulated." Is it a word? I don't care. I get to my feet, smooth my skirt, and step into a large room with high ceilings. I walk down a grand staircase. It's princess perfect, let me tell you, with polished wooden rails and more marble.

Tapestries hang from the wall and enormous woven rugs spread over the slatted floors. I spin in a slow circle. For the first time since arriving here, I feel like I've landed. Like I can rest. Breathe.

Antonio knocks lightly on the door. "Are you going to let me in?"

"Nah. I'm going to make myself at home." I open the door with a flourish and a smile.

"You're welcome to stay."

"My mama raised me right, but thank you."

He smirks and strides toward the open layout kitchen, immediately pulling out pots and pans, lighting burners, and chopping garlic.

"So is this what a busboy budget can get you around here? If so, I need to look into London real estate."

"No, it belongs to my cousin's friend."

"Ah, family discount."

"Something like that," he mutters, tightlipped about his family situation. Maybe I'm better off not knowing what the last name *Moretti* means here in Europe.

My stomach growls. "What can I do to help?"

"Watch the water boil."

"You know what they say about a watched pot..."

His dark eyes flicker with amusement. "It gets you to slow down. Enjoy the moment."

"Oh, that's a good one. I was going to say—"

He stuns me with his gaze. "I know what you were going to say. You Americans always go so fast. In Italy, we take it slow."

"Except this is England. And what about Ferraris, Maseratis, and Lamborghinis? Just to name a few Italian sports cars."

He lets out a deep chuckle.

While I watch the water, someone knocks on the door.

Antonio hollers, "It's open."

"Oh, now you forget to lock it. What if it's Jesse?"

He answers with a laugh as if to say that hooligan wouldn't dare breach these walls to *extract* revenge. Then again, he knew *the watched pot never boils* saying. Maybe his English is better than he's letting on.

A woman with long black hair and a red eyelet dress enters. She kisses Antonio on both cheeks. Then a woman with espadrilles and legs as long as the Thames follows after her. She does the same kiss-kiss thing. A couple, her with a yellow sundress and him with Converse parade in next. He carries a guitar.

They all chatter, thankfully in English, but they're very European. Hazel would fit in better with this crowd than me with my short stature and country denim style.

Antonio asked if I had a boyfriend, but I never queried with the obvious follow-up question. Does he have a girlfriend *or two*?

"This is Colette from South Carolina." He plants his hand on my low back like he's showing off a prize on a game show.

I give a meager wave. I mean, what else am I supposed to do with that introduction? I could bring out the tap shoes, but I think I'd get laughed off the stage.

He introduces Athena—of course, that's her name—and Willow with the long legs. Then Clive and Clementine—the couple.

While Antonio cooks they catch up, discussing fancy things like trips to Monte Carlo and polo matches.

"Where'd you two meet?" Clementine asks.

I shift uncomfortably.

"Funny story," Antonio says and proceeds to humiliate me. Not really, but the fountain, bridge, and everything else leave me feeling like a mermaid out of water. I know the saying is *fish out of water* but cut me some slack, I'm surrounded by nymphs here.

"You kissed her to trick the cop?" Athena says with a wry smile. Except her lips are so plump and perfect and pink I imagine Antonio kissing her. She's Italian and gorgeous from head to toe. I've gathered that they've known each other for a long time.

I'm not the kind of girl to blush. Nope. Being raised in the south made me immune to red cheeks. It's an adaptation. But they warm now and it's not because it's heating up in the kitchen.

How far is that bridge from here? I'd like to crawl under it.

"What brought you to London, anyway?" Willow asks.

"A bucket list," Antonio answers for me.

This piques their interest. As Antonio sets the table, they inquire about all the places I want to visit, telling me the best hotels, restaurants, and hidden spots on the route.

Antonio takes the seat next to me. We dig into a delicious dish of what he calls *pasta bianca*—white sauce with garlic, asparagus, parmesan, and fungi—I don't ask questions and not because mushrooms are slimy. Likely, his cultured friends will make me feel about an inch tall. Maybe I'm an elf or a sprite. A fairy? They're pretty small. It's not intentional, but they're just so fancy and put together, but in a casual way. It's hard to explain.

However, as I chew, bliss at the deliciousness bumps up against this bummer of a trip. "Antonio, this is slap your grandma delicious," I exclaim because I cannot help myself.

The room falls quiet, not even with a clink of silverware against tableware.

I wave my hands, panicked. "I don't mean your grandma. Or mine. God rest her soul. It's a saying. A southern saying," I mumble, realizing I've just proved how country I am.

They all laugh but not at me. Instead, they list things that are slap your grandma delicious—brie, pizza Napoletana, pavlova, and naan bread. Apparently, they got the joke.

As we continue to talk about traveling and I fill my belly with the warm meal, I settle in. Get more comfortable. As glasses refill, Clive takes out his guitar. We listen and sing along to some Beatles songs we all know.

Antonio's arm slides along the top of the chair behind me. While they talk, I think about the way he rushed to my defense earlier. I was in public, broad daylight, I could've gotten out of the situation just fine. Probably.

But it was nice to have someone in my corner. Nice to have Antonio there.

Or rather, here. By my side.

The evening continues, filled with laughter, warmth, and authenticity that I mistakenly took as haughtiness. I gaze from the new faces to the unfamiliar room with its high ceilings and ornate woodwork to Antonio.

A dusting of stubble.

Chiseled jaw.

Strong chin.

Dark eyes.

There's a sliver of space between forgetting about Marcus being gone and remembering what brought me here. I don't know which is worse.

Until Clive asks, "So why'd you make the bucket list?"

The room is so warm and I am so comfortable, I consider the truth. I don't know them. I'll never see them again. Jesse talked about freedom. To me, the truth is freedom just like when I told Mama about the mug.

"My husband and I made the list when we were in high school."

They all lean in. I'm suddenly the most interesting thing on the continent. The eighth wonder of the world.

"I thought you said you weren't married." Antonio's voice has a slight edge to it.

"I'm not." Yes, my finger tells a different story, but I brought the ring more so I could have Marcus with me.

Five sets of eyes jerk to the ring on my finger. Like before, I touch it self-consciously.

"I had a high school sweetheart. We were in love and got married after we graduated. I was going to college. He went into the military. We couldn't afford a honeymoon and we'd always talked about traveling so we made a bucket list of all the places we wished to visit. We started saving. Three months later he died in an accident."

Saying the words now, to these strangers, has no effect. At least none they can see. No tremble in my chin. No tears. I'm like one of the statues in the hotel this morning. Was that this morning? Yet, inside, there are splinters, fissures, broken parts. I've learned to hold them together. Mostly.

"So you're taking this trip to honor him? That's beautiful," Willow says.

I turn to Antonio. "I've never told anyone before."

Athena gets up and folds me into her arms. She whispers, "I'm a widow too."

When we draw apart, I realize that this gathering and meal has fed my soul more than the trip to Buckingham Palace—the first stop on the bucket list.

"Where to next?" Antonio asks.

I pass him the list.

"Amsterdam, a couple of the Scandinavian cities, Paris." He nods as he reads.

Willow practically launches out of her seat. "You should go together. Antonio can be your tour guide. He's traveling too."

I squint, looking around the room. "Looks like you're living...not traveling"

"You didn't tell her?" Clementine asks.

Antonio lifts and lowers a shoulder. "I'm looking for my mother."

"Or maybe you two were looking for each other," Athena says in her sultry, suggestive way.

At least I think so. She has a thick Italian accent. It's also suddenly loud in here as the others chirp about how perfect this setup is. Antonio can continue to look for his mother with a second set of eyes and see the bucket list items with a new set of eyes.

As for me, there's an overall keen concern for my safety.

"You can be her bodyguard. Make sure she doesn't fall in with more rabble," Clive says.

"I'm not hapless."

Clementine pats my hand. "Of course not."

I may as well be with Catherine, Hazel, Lottie, and Minnie. It's like my friends back in the states morphed into the European versions of themselves—except Hazel, she's always been sophisticated and worldly.

It's after midnight before everyone goes home. Antonio and Clive talk about jamming with their guitars soon. Of course, Antonio plays guitar. He's quite the renaissance man.

Willow passes me a piece of paper. "You dropped this when you took out the bucket list."

This time my cheeks burn. It's the *love list* Hazel and Minnie made while we were in the cafe when they came up with this ridiculous trip. Did she read it? I want to explain, but as she flounces out the door, she smirks, and says, "You may have already found what you're looking for."

But I'm not looking. This trip is about stepping into the past. Then as the door closes, leaving me alone with Antonio, I can't help but wonder if I'm looking at the future.

He offers to walk me to the hotel. I offer to help him clean up. It's like neither one of us want the night to end.

"I'll just call a cab."

"I can give you a ride."

"Do you have a car?"

"No." Here comes that smoldering, mischievous smile of his.

My eyes bulge. "Were you planning to steal one?"

His eyes sparkle with his smile. "Such a criminal mind. No, I would borrow my neighbor's."

"Borrow," I say, emphasizing the quotes with my first two fingers. Like how Jesse borrowed the phone charger?

Antonio wraps his hand around mine and then studies the ring. "You're a widow. I'm so sorry."

"It's been a long time. Over ten years." My throat feels thick, but at the same time flutters fill my belly. "I guess I want some closure."

He shakes his head. "The people we love never truly leave us even if they're not with us anymore."

"I just need some space from it. Sometimes it feels so heavy. Like it's dragging me down."

He nods like he understands to a degree. Maybe because of his search for his mom.

"I can help you look if you'd like," I offer.

His lips twitch with a smile. "I can promise not to steal anything."

Except for my heart. There's a fair chance he could make off with that.

CHAPTER 8
TONIGHT, TONIGHT
ANTONIO

For a minute there, it looked like Colette was going to leave with the others, but she lowers onto the couch. Perhaps it's from the weight of her grief. For a long moment, she looks around the room.

"Are you going to try to steal my art?" I ask, joking. That's more my father's line of work, but you can never be too careful.

"More like your leftovers. I love—your cooking. The meal." She presses her hand over her eyes and then her fingers part and she peeks at me.

I ignore what that does to my pulse. My brain fires a warning shot.

"I meant...I was thinking...I just don't want to rush into, um, restaurants. Nothing like a home cooked meal."

Deciphering her bashful yet flirty code might require Sherlock Holmes' assistance. Baker Street isn't far from here.

"I have more pots of water you can watch boil. It's good practice," I say.

She cracks a smile.

I lean forward, resting my elbows on my knees and decide to take a risk—mostly for her sake. I wouldn't want the turnip truck to break down. "I don't want to push you into anything like your friends did, but would you like to travel together?"

Her gaze lifts to mine as if she's been thinking about this ever since the others suggested it. "It would be nice to have someone to keep me out of trouble. And I was serious, I can help you look for your mother."

I lean back on the couch, cradling my head in my hands. I hadn't fully considered that.

"Or not," she says when I fail to answer.

My attention is skyward as though I'll find direction there. The truth is I don't think I'll ever find her, especially if she doesn't want to be found. I pass Colette the journal and then lean back on the couch. "That is the only thing I have that belonged to her. You can look inside."

A little wrinkle forms between Colette's eyebrows as she turns it over carefully in her hands.

"I've read it backward and forward, a dozen times at least. I thought it would provide clues. All I've found are dead ends." And that there is my biggest fear. That I'll never know her.

"Are you sure you don't mind if I read it? Maybe I'll pick up something you missed."

I jut my chin in the affirmative. "My father's family tree is strong. Proud. Not a branch unaccounted for—except Alonzo, but that's another story. For the first twenty-seven years of my life, I thought my father's wife was my mother, Imelda. It turns out he'd cheated. When my mother went to him, telling him about the pregnancy and that it was a boy, he turned her away. Kept the baby. Needed someone to carry on the family legacy. The woman I called Mama almost my whole life went along with it." I scoff. Disgusted, disappointed.

Colette clutches the diary to her chest. "How tragic. I am so sorry."

"Dramatic, more like. That's the Moretti way. I grew up thinking I shared the same mother as my sisters. Eventually, they had more kids—presumably. Two sons."

"How many Morettis are there?"

"Six of us. My brother found the journal. Put two and two together. Called me out as an illegitimate son. I felt so deceived." I scrub my hand down my face. "Despite how tough my father is and how many goons surround him, he's lucky that I don't—never mind. It's in the past. I'm here now."

Colette's eyes widen with fear...or is it curiosity?

I worry that I've said too much. Too soon. Turned the burner up too fast. "We can test the water here. Finish up your London bucket list first."

"Considering how refined and cultured your friends are you may laugh at my next stop."

My lips twitch. "I saw the list." I also saw her adorable, playfully printed underwear but leave that part out. Before you come at me, I didn't mean to look and they fit no differently than a bathing suit bottom—the modest kind and not the European style if you're feeling judgy.

"It's silly and I know I'm a little old, but I don't care." A bashful smile nudges the corners of her lips as she looks at me from under long lashes.

"If you're talking about Harry Potter, they were the first books I read in English. I'll take you to see Platform 9 3/4."

She squeals and bounces in her seat.

I can't suppress my smile and get to my feet. "We'll bring umbrellas this time just in case. I found a pink one like Hagrid's around here somewhere."

She blinks a few times. "You mean you want to go right now?"

"Less likely for there to be a crowd. Plus it's on the way to your hotel."

It's not.

But I want to spend more time with Colette. Hear about life in South Carolina and Manhattan and if she believes in unicorns.

I crook my elbow for her to take.

"Are we going to disapparate?" Hope fills her voice as if it's something we might just be able to do.

"Magic flue powder," I say, also referencing the story.

We wander past St. Pancras Station, and I explain how the filmmakers used the exterior in the second movie, but the genuine article is King's Cross, which isn't far away. I share all kinds of cool facts about the series that I've gathered since living here. We try to out-nerd each other as our laughter spills across the damp and sleeping streets.

Usually, the vacuous station bustles with people moving in every direction. We locate a brick wall marked *Platform 9 3/4* with a luggage cart lodged halfway in. We take turns posing for photos, but even with the excitement we share, I can't help fear that I'm at risk. Kinks and knots form in my chest at what this woman could do to me.

When we get outside, Colette says, "So where have you looked for your mother? Catch me up to speed."

As we walk, I tell her about my travels, searching for my mother.

"Do you remember her at all?"

I shift my head subtly from side to side as if by denying my response a memory might appear.

"What can you tell me about her?"

"Her name is Kristy. Her mother, my grandmother, was Moira. They were from just outside London," I say even though I haven't been able to locate anything else about my grandmother. "My mother liked flowers and hated cooking, I think. She had a wandering spirit. Loved to travel."

"What did she look like?"

"There's a photo that was torn in half, taped inside the journal. I think the other half had my father in it. Her hair is a few shades lighter than mine and she wore it swept to the side. We have the same eyes."

"She sounds pretty," Colette's voice is small, reverent.

"She's older now," I answer, doing the math.

A dark thought pushes through the gratitude for Colette's encouragement, for trying. What if my mother didn't love me? I push the answer away.

"Thanks for bringing me there." She points over her shoulder at the station. "Marcus and I had this big dream, all through high school we'd talk about trips we'd take to visit all the continents, circumnavigating the world. But then we narrowed it down. Figured we'd start in Europe. We'd already gone to Canada for a class trip and Mexico for spring break."

"I went to the U.S. once."

She nods like that's not very impressive. But it's all relative, I suppose.

"Marcus wanted to plan everything out. He wasn't a wanderer."

"Sometimes we find what we're looking for by accident and when we least expect it, you know?" This might be the truest thing I've ever said.

"If you do find her, what will you say?"

The question catches me off guard and I stop. "Hello," I guess.

Colette laughs. "That's a start."

But my heart knows. I'd ask, *Why'd you leave? Where'd you go?* I'd ask her to fill in the gaps between then and now.

"Do you remember how Luna Lovegood said lost things always have a way of turning up?" she asks, referencing Harry Potter again.

The evening light blurs the edges of the surrounding buildings, houses, and trees—and my resolve to follow Colette's lead, to go slow, and most importantly listen to the alarm bells in my head when she looks up at me through her fringed lashes. Her eyes sparkle. Her lips are so perfectly full.

My insides pop and sizzle. "We should get you to the hotel before dawn."

Her laugh is raspy as though sleep is a silly idea. "Or we could watch the sunrise."

I glance at my watch. "And have a fry up."

"Huh?"

"Eggs, sausage, and potatoes, a proper breakfast."

And that is how we end up talking all night in Hyde Park. We only stop talking as the sun pulls itself over the horizon, painting with watercolors in the sky.

There's something beautiful and enchanted about this particular morning. I want to capture it on film, but I'm afraid nothing could properly convey the way I feel with Colette. Maybe what I've been looking for is closer than I realized.

After breakfast, we wander back through Hyde Park as it comes alive with picnics, kids flying kites, couples in rowboats, dogs frolicking, and everyone enjoying the splendor of a rainless summer day in the city.

Colette boldly approaches a few groundskeepers and strangers, showing them the photo of my mother, describing her. But all we get in reply are shakes of the head, shrugs, and profuse apologies.

We rest on the grass, me with my head cradled in my hands and her with her head cradled in the nook by chest and arm. I'm swept up in my surroundings, in the greenness of the grass, the pops of color in the ornamental gardens, and the fragrance of the flowers...in Colette.

"Is it time for tea?" she asks sleepily, pulling me from my thoughts, but dropping me squarely into another one. "Or a nap?"

"We never did get you to your hotel."

"Sleeping is overrated. Except I really could doze off right here."

I recall her close call under the bridge. "We'd better get you to the hotel before they give away your room."

As we stroll down the street, Colette says, "My mother loves tea. She collects teacups and saucers, and fanciful teapots arranged neatly on shelves in the dining room of our house. I wasn't allowed to touch those. She usually drank out of mugs, never using the nicer sets. The tea stained the inside of her favorite one from using it so much. On one side was the British Flag and on the other was the image of a dog, a Yorkie. It was a floof." She smiles fondly.

"We had shepherds. Guard dogs."

"We were a no pets family. My sister is allergic. Allergic to life, more like. Want to talk about a princess?" Colette mumbles. "Anyway, I broke the mug when I was a kid."

"You could send her a replacement."

"Thing is, she doesn't know I'm here."

I halt. "What?"

"I didn't tell my parents about the trip. They'd have tried to stop me."

I wince. "Well, they probably want to keep track of the turnip truck."

Colette laughs. "Where can I get a mug? Preferably with some tea in it because I am exhausted."

"We'll get tea and then a nap for you."

"Can we continue our bucket listing later though? I'm having fun."

I sling my arm around her. I've met a lot of people in my travels but no one that's made me want to stop for longer than a little while. To go slow. "I'm having fun too, but I have to go to work soon, so you'll have to swing by for dinner. I'll make sure you get a double basket of chips." I wink.

She backs away and blanches. "What? The lady didn't touch them."

I chuckle. "I'm sure Justine would like to see you. She was worried. Thought you were a wanderer and that you might end up falling in with some hooligans. Maybe passing out under a bridge."

"I'm sure she'd like to see *you.*" Colette winks at me. Or maybe blinks because we're passing a shop with a giant Yorkie on the sign.

Etched on the glass window is the head of a giant Yorkshire

terrier. The sign above reads *Yorkie's at Five. Established: Yorkshire 1892 and London 1982.*

We go inside. I inhale the bitter and comforting scent of tea. Sure enough, against one wall is an assortment of coffee mugs bearing the resemblance of someone's beloved pup and the English flag.

Colette brings it to the clerk and while she wraps it, Colette asks, "Have you worked here long?"

"It'll be two years next month," she says with sigh.

"Is there someone here who's been here longer? My mother visited, must've been over thirty years ago." Colette glances at me. "I wonder if our moms met—it would've been around the same time."

She's sweet, but that's a stretch. "Unlikely."

"As unlikely as you and me running into each other four times?"

"Fair point."

A man wearing tawny trousers, a tan shirt, and sparse, brown hair emerges from the backroom. He's the personification of tea. "May I help you?"

"My mother came here a long time ago. I'm wondering if there's a chance you may have seen this woman too." She shows him the photo from the journal.

He shakes his head apologetically. "I'm sorry, miss. I inherited the shop from my aunt about five years ago. Along with," he juts his chin toward a photo of the Yorkie. "All twelve of her dogs."

"Oh wow," Colette says as if not sure whether to offer condolences or to adopt one of the dogs.

"Thank you, sir." I'm touched that Colette inquired but also disappointed. I foolishly hoped some of the magic we've been experiencing might have rubbed off.

I walk Colette to the hotel. At the entrance, she lifts onto her toes and kisses me on one cheek and then swipes to the other side and loses her footing. I grip her hands and she leans into the other cheek.

"It looked so fancy when Athena did it."

I don't think I've stopped smiling since yesterday. This woman is going to be responsible for my cheeks freezing in place. "She has a lot of practice." A moment too late, I realize how that sounds.

Colette's expression shadows. "Oh. Well, thanks for the rescue, the dinner, and the bucket listing."

"Grazie," I say, thanking her in Italian. I lean in, ready to kiss on properly on both cheeks.

She shrinks back. "Thanks for what? Watching the water boil?"

My brain pipes up, reminding me to keep my distance. It would be so easy to fall for her. "Something like that."

"See you later. I want that double basket of fries."

"Ciao," I say.

But I don't see her later. Not when I pick up another shift and not when I down my third shot of espresso. Not when I wander back to my flat. This disappointment slices deeper than not finding my mother.

Brain: Told you so.

Me: I should go look for her. Check the hotel. Make sure she's not in any kind of trouble.

Brain: You're already looking for one woman and that's hard enough.

This time, I'm silent.

CHAPTER 9
THEATER IN THE FOUND
COLETTE

I sleep well into the next day. This room isn't as posh as the Four Seasons, but the blackout curtains do the trick. At last, my mind is clear of the jet lag fuzz and I feel like the Princess and the Pea minus the produce.

I'm about to call Antonio and apologize, but we never traded numbers. A little twinge inside tips me off to the fact that it's not the worst thing. After all, why am I in London? To focus on the bucket list. Not an Italian that makes delicious pasta and keeps me out all night.

Grandmama would not approve.

Instead, I dial Hazel. Even though I'm not quite as ticked off as I was yesterday, I have no qualms about waking her up at four a.m. eastern standard time.

She answers with a groggy, "Hello."

"Top o' the morning to you. Oh, wait. Wrong country."

"Colette, do you realize what time it is?"

"Sure do, Hazel. Time to tell you off for connecting me with Jesse. He was a walking, talking disaster. *He,* and yes I'm emphasizing the fact that *he* was a male because that was not specified in the contract—"

"Whoa, whoa. Slow down. Why are you so mad? Jesse's great."

"I was expecting a polite British woman in coordinating knits and flats. Your doppelganger in the very least. Maybe someone with a sense of humor because that's a prerequisite to be your friend. But honey, I am not laughing."

"You're honey-ing me?" I can tell that got her attention, and she sat up because her voice is less garbled.

"I sure am, darlin'." My southern accent comes on thick. "If he's your best childhood friend, I'd hate to know your enemies." At that, I tell her exactly what happened.

At each moment of punctuation, she interjects with a, "No," of disbelief.

"Yes, Hazel. Yes, that bad. That insane. That roguish."

"Jesse, dangerous? I can't fathom it. He was such a nice kid. Good manners. A bit cheeky, but who isn't?"

"Then there's the rake."

"Like the garden tool?"

"No, like in historical romance. A real Romeo."

"Shakespeare?"

"Italian. Antonio."

"Have you been reading Catherine's books?"

Now that I have my wits about me, I'm having second thoughts about the blur of the garlic and cheese-heavy meal with Antonio, the romance of strolling through the midnight streets and watching the sunrise. "A real-life ladies' man. You should've seen Athena and Willow and Clementine. I have no doubt he dated them."

"Do tell." I have her full attention now and describe the details of meeting Antonio multiple times and then last night.

"I knew it. I knew you'd find love."

"Love?" I croak.

"You say the word like you picked up a soggy piece of cardboard out of a gutter."

I want to deny this but cannot. Instead, I change the subject. "Nice hotel choice by the way."

"You can thank Maxwell. But don't even try to get out of this, missus. You met Antonio at the Eros fountain in Piccadilly? That place is legendary for making true love matches."

I laugh. "If there's a god or goddess of love, which there is not, you'd also think there'd be a department specifically for making sure people who clash and aren't meant to be together don't meet—such as Jesse and me. There isn't, thereby proving your theory false."

"Good one, detective. What about Cupid?"

"Then there'd be an anti-Cupid. And, what's more, why would an adorable little cherub use violence with that bow and arrow to win over hearts? Seems barbaric."

"Oh, you're just fired up. Feeling the sting of love's keen arrow, huh? Soon, it'll smooth over and you'll feel fine."

I harrumph.

"When you come home, I owe you a batch of double chocolate cookies because I miss you and one kind of chocolate isn't enough."

"That's so sweet, but I know you'll make Maxwell bake them so it doesn't count. And don't try to win me over with chocolate."

"What about garlic?"

Despite my frustration and disappointment, I do miss her and my other friends. I wish they were here.

"There may not be a god or goddess of love or Cupid, but there is a Hazel. Me. I wasn't wrong about Catherine and Kellan."

"You're sly, bringing it back around to your quest for everyone to have a happily ever after. You haven't met Antonio."

"You're a good judge of character." She's trying to flatter me and get back in my good graces.

"And Jesse is proof that you are not." I huff.

"Ouch. He must've changed. Seemed the same in our texts.

Come to think of it, his address is the former residence of a member of parliament. I thought he'd found success but working at a museum parking garage can't pay that well."

"He's probably a squatter, living in squalor and involved in petty street crimes to get by. He mentioned something about a palace and hinted at robbing Buckingham."

"Oh dear. Maybe he needs help. An intervention."

"I think he's well past that. But I appreciate your hopeful attitude. Next time you come to England, pay him a surprise visit. Just don't go on a crime spree. He's persuasive."

"Noted. Get a paper. A pen. I want you to write something down," Hazel says.

I grab the little pad of paper and the nicely weighted pen off the desk across the room. "Shoot."

"I've been carrying pieces of my broken heart around for years and vow to let each of the stops on the bucket list stitch it back together."

I blink a few times, rereading the words Hazel dictated. I toss the pen across the desk. "Oh, you're cunning."

"It must have something to do with the mean streets of London." I hear a wink in her voice. "Now, I want you to go find that Italian. Take him along on your adventures. See what happens. You may just fall in love."

That's exactly what I'm afraid of.

After saying goodbye to Hazel, I take an absurdly long shower, after which I use all the available spa products in the room. I slip on a sundress and a pair of tennis shoes. I smooth the list containing a few more stops in London.

Consulting the itinerary, I have a couple more days here and then it's off to Amsterdam where English isn't the first language. Maybe having Antonio along would be a good thing. Don't want to fall off the turnip truck again.

As I step into the silvery sunshine of London mid-morning, I grab a smoothie—feeling very independent like I did when I first moved to Manhattan. I went from country mouse to city girl.

Now, I'm a woman of the world. I want to sashay down the street and tell everyone I pass, but that would only serve to highlight the fact that I am not very worldly. Not like Athena and Willow and Clementine.

Nope. I'm Colette—sweet, sassy, and a lover of Shakespeare. I discretely consult the map and memorize the route to the Globe Theater. In high school, I was really into the Bard...and Harry Potter. Those were my picks for the bucket list. Marcus wanted to see Churchill's War Room and loads of other imperial-type spots, but they didn't feel like romantic-ish bucket list items.

I get a ticket for the tour, a performance of *A Winter's Tale*, which is welcome because if I didn't know better, I'd think I was trudging through a swamp. I didn't time it properly to have tea at Swan's, but I do pick up a container of Midsummer's Night Tea and a key chain at the souvenir shop, feeling very smug—when I was a kid my mother never gave me spending money for field trips and I was the only kid who'd leave without a little paper loot bag.

After the *brilliant* show—I'm a quick study and learn words like that, *cheeky*, and *fancy* are used in abundance here—I'm hungry and wander over to a familiar pub. Do I fancy Antonio, I mean chips? Yes, yes I do.

I find the place I was supposed to go to yesterday. I'm a day late and prepare an apology for Antonio.

Justine greets me with less warmth than the first time I came in. I'll be sure to pay and leave her a big tip this time.

After I place my order, I ask, "Is Antonio here?"

"No. He quit." Disappointment hollows out her voice.

I'm seated, otherwise, I'd stagger backward.

"He came in yesterday for his shift, pleased as punch, boasting about how he was planning a big trip. He's taken little jaunts here and there looking for his mother, mind, but this was going to be epic, he said." She hangs her head. "As time passed, he seemed upset. Distracted really. It's a shame. Best looking busboy, er, man, we've had in a while." She mumbles the last bit.

Every time I hear someone approach, I glance over my shoulder. But he doesn't show up. Why would he? I was supposed to meet him last night. I fell asleep. He must be crushed...and unemployed.

When the bill arrives, I leave Justine triple the amount I normally would. Just as I'm about to leave, I ask, "By any chance, do you have Antonio's number or a way to contact him?"

"The manager would, but she stepped out. It's slow today. Anyway, I never got up the nerve to ask him for his number." She flutters her lashes. "I'm a few years older than him, but I don't blame you for taking a fancy."

I smile. "Um, thanks."

Justine bites her lip and then pulls a slim brown paper bag from her apron. "I was holding onto this hoping Antonio will come back to collect his last check. The boss usually mails them. But if you see him, someone left this earlier." Her gaze dims with guilt.

It's the size and shape of a book. I clasp it to my chest feeling hopeful—maybe I'll find him after all. "Thank you," I'll make sure he gets it."

But how to find a handsome Italian? I try to trace my way back through the quaint and cobbled streets where I think his rental was, but we'd entered through an alley and they're all identical. Plus, it's dodgy to go creeping behind buildings even in the broad daylight.

I leaf through our conversations, trying to grasp anything that would point me to where I might find him. Then I remember the location of Willow's shop. If you guessed it's called *Willow,* you'd be correct. I type it into my phone and follow the directions to an upscale clothing boutique.

She's not in and after hassling the aloof worker, I'm no better than when I started. I leave a note with my number but by the look on the gal's face, it'll accidentally fall into the bin. I can't help that I forgot a hair tie and my blond locks hang in frizzy hanks, getting caught between my torso and arm. Yes, fine, it's getting stuck in my armpits. Gross. I know.

I sit on a curb, wracking my brain and imagining a little cartoon Antonio wearing a red cap like in the *Where's Waldo* books when I was a kid. Antonio is much cuter.

Our paths crossed a total of four times. I've missed Antonio three times so far today—the pub, trying to find his house, and stopping by Willow's shop. According to this logic, we'll meet again. The fourth time.

But that could be today or in thirty years.

I pull out the brown bag Justine gave me to find a copy of *A Midsummer's Night Dream*. It's tatty and the edges are frayed. I part the yellowed pages and find the name Kristy Nichols on the inside cover. I launch to my feet.

It belonged to his mother. I must get this to Antonio. I pull out a bookmark for a bookstore called the *Logophile: a new and used book shop for lovers of words*.

Renewed with hope, I consult the map and rush down the sidewalk toward Wickworth Row. The breeze from the Thames blows away the remaining humidity from the day and hastens me forward.

When I reach the building with brown trim and a white, gold, and black sign, I wilt. It's shuttered for the night. I cup my hands around the sides of my face and peer in the window. It's a booklover's paradise with both tidy shelves and stacks of books that look like they could tip over from heavy footfalls. No sign of a cat lazing around, but I bet it's in there somewhere.

I tap the book against my thigh and catch the reflection of someone behind me. I brace for Jesse, ready to *extract* revenge for embarrassing him yesterday.

Instead, a tall, well-built Italian stands at my back. His dark lashes frame those mysterious eyes of his—they make me crave chocolate.

He blinks slowly as if seeing me for the first time then brushes his hair from his face.

Even though I haven't run in a few minutes, I inhale and exhale like I'm still trying to catch my breath. "Justine said this was left for you. I've been trying to find you. I'm sorry I didn't show up last night. I over—"

He takes a step closer to me, reaching out. "I'll admit. I thought the worst. But then realized you probably took a very long nap."

I nod rapidly as I pass him the book.

Our hands brush. A pleasant zing travels from my skin, up my arm, landing right in the middle of my chest.

"Look inside," I say at more of a whisper than I mean.

But his eyes remain on me. "*Buona fortuna.*" And his smile is irrepressible.

Mine too.

CHAPTER 10
HERMIA & LYSANDER
ANTONIO

Maybe this is luck, a small miracle, or a piece of a larger plan unfolding because it turns out lost things—or people—do have a way of turning up. Maybe I'll find my mother yet.

But back to the blond beauty in front of me. I thought Colette had disappeared. Fled. Decided she wasn't interested in this mopey Italian.

Her smile lifts to her eyes. "Open it," she repeats, gesturing to the book.

Yes, my quest to find my mother has driven me all over the continent, but for one fleeting moment, the feeling that I've found exactly what—and who—I've actually been looking for overwhelms me.

Her expectant expression snaps me to the book in my hands, a worn copy of *A Midsummer's Night Dream*. Printed inside the cover is the name Kristy Nichols.

A little thrill of excitement shoots through me. "This was her favorite of Shakespeare's works. How'd you get this?"

"Justine said someone left it for you."

I pull out my phone and scroll through my emails. "I'd received an email from the bookshop owner that he'd found something for me." Buried in our exchanges, I realize he'd said he'd leave it at the restaurant.

"In that case, good thing I found you. I've traipsed all over the city today, starting at The Globe Theater with Shakespeare and ending it here with Shakespeare."

"But the day isn't over yet." I flutter the brittle and dusty pages of the book. "How'd you like the Globe?"

"It was grand. Have you been?"

"To every inch of the place." The skills I learned when I was younger helped me gain access to the restricted areas of the building. "My mother performed there in a production of *A Midsummer's Night Dream* years ago. She played Titiana. I thought I'd hit the zachpot."

Colette chuckles. "The expression is the jackpot, but go on. Sounds promising."

My lips quirk. "I got a couple of dead-end leads, except that she'd been friends with the owner of a bookshop. An older fellow now, but he recalled her fondly." I waggle my eyebrows suggestively. "She left on her travels after a while, leaving him with nothing other than her copy of Shakespeare's book and the memory of the greatest kiss of his life. TMI. He kept the book, but it must've taken him a while to find."

"Well, that's double *buona fortuna* then because I got you this." She dangles a Globe Theater Keychain between us.

She tells me more about her trip to the theater and then trying to find me. "But I missed tea time."

"I know just the place to go." I glance down at the book glad to have it but fairly certain it's another dead end.

"It looks well-read," Colette says softly as if she can read my mind, my disappointment.

"I wasn't expecting a map or a trail of breadcrumbs, but where could she be?" It's a pointless question that I should stop asking.

"The chances of me stopping by the pub, Justine giving me the book, and then you and I meeting at this precise time and in this precise place are slim. I cannot fathom the odds." But then she gives me the warmest, most reassuring smile. "But if you've read that story, then you know that a life filled with words is magical."

At that, a cabbie honks as another car cuts him off. We both startle from the moment.

"Or life can be chaotic," I mutter.

Colette chuckles like she knows that all too well. "Do you know what goes with tea? Cookies. Or biscuits, as they call them here. Shortbread, chocolate, double chocolate, oatmeal, gingerbread, lemon crinkle, peanut butter, sugar…Mmm. Sugar cookies."

I check the time and we take the least direct way to our destination, partly because it's still a bit early and partly because I want as much time with Colette as I can have. Like with my mother, I teeter on the edge of fear that she might take flight—that I might. We stroll along the Thames. I breathe in the damp river air, pulling it down, and letting that thought drip into the river.

"Justine said you quit your job at the pub."

I balance on another edge—the truth.

"I want to travel with you. But I also want to be careful."

"Why's that? Because I have dangerous friends." She cuts the sarcasm in half with a laugh. "For the record, Jesse and I are not and were not friends."

I wag my outstretched pointer finger between us. "But you and me? That's what I want to be careful with."

She nods slowly. "Right. Of course. That makes perfect sense. Me too."

But does it? Does it align with what I want? What I feel?

No, but it does match with what I fear.

She clears her throat. "While we're on the topic of records, I do not have a boyfriend."

I recall asking her if she had a boyfriend and tuck away this fact for later. The little ember of hope inside me sticks its tongue out at my brain as if it scored a point against my better judgment.

"Speaking of records, I know just where to go."

We walk to Leonard Street, lined with cars, trash bins, and a crowd of people in front of a blue storefront labeled with a small sign that says *The AV Club*. The unmistakable lure of freshly brewed espresso draws me into the queue.

"This place makes the best tea and has an old turntable with a massive record collection. People sign up for hour-long spots and play music for the patrons."

"That's cool. Seeing the famous sites is amazing, but I like these little hidden parts of London too. That's one of my favorite parts of living in Manhattan. I'm always finding new places to check out. You should visit sometime."

That reminder that her home isn't here sets the clock ticking. At some point, she'll leave. It isn't today, thankfully, but it will happen.

The line moves forward.

"Were you there?" asks a girl in front of us in line.

"Where?" Colette replies, confused.

"Here." The girl has a stud in her nose and pink hair. "The show, last night. You should come to the one tonight. The Loop is playing. Saw them last month—the guitar player is—" She fans herself then turns back to her friend. "And you too. I'm not taking a no for an answer this time. They truly have the best bands play," she says, gesturing to the AV Club and stepping inside as the line moves up again. "The Loop do originals and covers, but get everyone singing along, forget that polite shoegazing nonsense."

Adverts hang in the window for music—including the band from last night, Roscoe's Tulip and The Loop, tonight—, as well as an art show with a nineties theme, and Pongapalooza, a ping-pong competition.

"Do you want to go?" I ask Colette. "I know the promoter. We can probably get tickets."

She nibbles her lip and then as if deciding on the spot, says, "I guess I know what we're doing tonight. I like the idea of traveling like a local. I should start my own blog."

That simple word, *we*, brightens the ember inside. "With a glowing recommendation like that, how could we say no."

The girl in front of us smiles. "You won't be disappointed."

When we get to the front of the line, Colette opts for tea and I stick with espresso.

Colette stares at the cookie display. "I'll take one of each of those."

The guy, wearing a nametag that says *Puck*, looks confused for a long moment.

"There are five kinds of cookies. They all look so good. I can't decide. I may have drooled a little, so I'll take one of each." Then she says to me, "Don't worry. I'll share."

"Name?" the barista asks so they can call out when the order is ready.

"Hermia and Lysander," Colette says in all seriousness.

The reference to *A Midsummer's Night Dream* must be lost on the guy named Puck. But not on me. My lips twitch with silent laughter.

We wait at the other end of the counter. The airy and open floor plan, the hodgepodge of tables and chairs, the plants, the art on the walls—some brick and others plaster—juxtaposes the account of the wild night the girl in line described with disco lights and loud music.

However, even now, the place is packed and all the tables are full.

When the barista calls our names, we weave through the café slash meeting space slash art gallery slash ping pong hall slash restaurant slash record shop.

At the very back, there's a recess in the wall shoved full of books near an empty table. I browse the spines: a few classics, some science fiction, titles I've never heard of, and a frayed binding printed with *A Midsummer's Night Dream*.

"Where are you?" I whisper.

"Right here," Colette says.

Our eyes meet for a fleeting moment. There's the spark again.

Is it time to stop looking for my mother and focus on the person I have found?

Colette takes a sip of tea. "I know you meant your mother. I understand the sadness. The longing." She still wears the wedding band around her finger. "But love once given is always in us, part of the fabric of who we are. Yet, it's bittersweet, to have the love but not the person."

But that's the thing. I don't know that my mother loved me. If she did, she would've stayed, right? Some words are hard for me to think, never mind say so I keep this hidden away.

Colette breaks an oatmeal raisin cookie in half. "Sometimes what we think we want turns out to be disappointing. Sometimes it's better to focus on what we have."

Her comment echoes what I've been thinking.

She passes half the cookie to me. Our fingers brush, sending that electric zing up my arm and to my chest where a little throb reminds me where my heart is.

"*Vacilando*." The word curls around my tongue.

In French, Colette says that the only other language she knows is French. But I think there's another language we're learning, one all our own. Then, also in French, she asks what *vacilando* means.

I call on my knowledge of the language. "It's a Spanish term for wandering when the experience of travel is more important than reaching the destination. Always going somewhere, but not minding whether or not you get there because you're where you are."

"Just a long, continuous journey. There is no end."

My brain tells me there will be though. In reckless defiance, I reply out loud. "But what we have is right now. The big this." I shake my hands emphatically.

Her eyes and smile sparkle. She switches back to English and says, "Yes. The big this and then that. Living right now and now and now."

She understands no matter the language.

When we're done, I leave the copy of *A Midsummer's Night Dream* on the table.

"Don't forget this," Colette says, passing it to me.

But I put it on the shelf with the other one. My disappointment in the book not moving me closer to my mother changes shape. I'm not giving up, not on hope, or love, or on someday finding my mother. But perhaps not looking so hard that I miss what's in front of me. "I understand now that the point of this search has been the adventure, and it's led me right here, to you."

She bumps me with her hip. "Be careful, Romeo. Those words might make me want to stick around."

"I hope so."

I incline my head and we're inches apart.

Her eyes sparkle and flit to the scar that slices through one of my eyebrows. "How'd that happen?"

My fingers lift to it. "That was another adventure. Amsterdam."

"That's on my bucket list."

"*Andiamo,*" I answer.

"Is that another Spanish term?"

I shake my head. "Italian. It means *let's go.*" I take her hand in a not-going-to-let-go kind of hold.

"Where do you want to go, Antonio?" she asks.

"With you, Colette." Excitement bubbles inside me, ricocheting around my stomach and my chest.

She squeezes back. "*Andiamo,*" she repeats.

CHAPTER 11
THE DUEL
COLETTE

Back outside, Leonard Street consists of quirky shops and eateries, scaffolding, and dirty brick. An old factory building, complete with a tall smokestack looms ahead, but instead of belching out soot, the somehow melodious duo of a guy playing bongo drums with a bagpiper dressed in a kilt issues from the entryway. A crowd listens, some people bobbing their heads. Beyond, stalls display everything from bicycles, to macarons, to boots.

We listen and then leave them with the rest of the cookies and a few coins.

As I glance up at the tall Italian with the tousled hair, devastating smile, and purposeful stride who holds my hand, *this* is the adventure. I feel like Hermia. Like there's no one I'd rather be with than Lysander.

We wind through the stalls as shopkeepers offer free samples and discounts. Others focus on their phones and still more do live demonstrations of the art that they sell in their little shops. There's every kind of food from Burmese to Bulgarian along with countless other smells and dishes that I don't recognize.

The humid air sticks to my skin and even though what I'm

doing right now wasn't on the bucket list, I can't help but feel like I'm exactly where I'm supposed to be.

After the sun sets in a cloudy haze, we return to the AV Club for the concert. The line is even longer than it was earlier.

Antonio stands nearly a head taller than many of the surrounding people. The eyes of women in the crowd flick to him and then to me as if gauging whether we're together.

Me too, sisters.

I don't blame them. Well, maybe a little bit. After all, jealousy is a central theme in *A Midsummer's Night Dream*. My eyes are on Antonio too. He's hot. Model hot. Sultry summer night hot. Hottie hot. I want him to look-at-me and only-me hot. I want his lips on mine hot.

My cheeks feel hot.

We bypass the line. Wearing a confident smile like he knows every woman in Europe loves him, Antonio says, "I texted with Izzy—the promoter. She said we can go right in."

She. The jealousy spikes again and gives me pause. Does it point to the depth of my feelings...and my insecurities? Or the very real fact that Antonio is well out of my reach, my league, and my stratosphere for that matter.

Once inside, a tall woman with spiky black hair and high heeled boots to match throws her arms around him. I'm guessing this is Izzy. She has urban sophistication and a smoky voice. Together, the two of them could be a living, breathing perfume ad like the kind on the wall in the Tube station.

I suddenly feel like the ittiest, bittiest country mouse there ever was. As she smooths her hand down his chest, jealousy makes my muscles stiffen and coil like a feral beast ready to protect what's mine. Never mind a mouse, more like lioness.

Whoa there, catwoman. I stagger back, surprised by my inner ferocity.

"There's another band, Mega, playing first. They're friends with the Loop so they arranged it as a surprise to the fans," Izzy says. "You'll love them."

Antonio's gaze floats to mine and his arm presses to my low back. "This is Colette."

Like the women outside, Izzy's eyes flick to mine in question.

Who am I to the swarthy Italian? A friend? A Friday night date? Something more?

I take a step closer to Antonio, possessively. Ready to fight off any other felines who try to edge in on my territory.

But is he mine?

Izzy's expression shifts quickly through disbelief to disregard because likely she has a line of men waiting to return their interest.

"Welcome, Colette. I hope you like it here. The AV Club came about when a group of friends got together. One loved art, another music, one food, books, and so forth. They mixed it up and created a collective of artistry. From the interior to the coffee to the events they host. They hired me because I'm the best."

The roar of people seems to echo her claim as the doors open, letting in the crowd.

"That's my cue to—" She points behind her. "Enjoy the show."

We find a spot upfront as the space fills in. The lights blink three times before everything falls dark except for the soft glow of twinkle lights festooning the edges of the ceiling. Antonio's hand finds mine and he squeezes. I flinch, but not because I reject the squeeze he gives me. Rather, because it's like lightning, brightening me from the inside.

Should I be concerned that even though it's been days, and not years, that we've known each other, it feels so right?

"This is my favorite part," he whisper-shouts.

"Have you seen them before?" I ask, expecting the band's show-stopping entrance.

"No, anticipation is my favorite part." I hear the smile in his voice. "Looking forward to things," he adds.

The hum in the room and the buzz between Antonio and me

make me understand what he means—the sliver of time between when I know something is going to happen and when it does.

His smile beams from his sun-kissed skin. Yet, his eyes dip heavily in a smolder. I return the smile, but mine is shaky, expectant, filled with yearning. If I'm not careful, I might drool again like I did when I saw those perfect cookies in the display earlier. Yes, I understand exactly what he means by anticipation.

Before I can think further, a single spotlight shines onto the stage. A woman with long hair, cascading down both sides of her face, strides into the center.

A tall guy wearing a hat steps in front of me, blocking my view. Without comment, Antonio grips my waist, and he switches spots with me so I can see.

The singer tucks her hair behind her ear and says, "Getting on stage never gets easier. Every time I think I might puke. Sometimes I do. But then—" Her accent is thick and I think she might be Eastern European or Russian.

Yes. I get what she means too. Well, not to that extreme, but every time Antonio's eyes land on me then drop to my lips, my stomach curls up, flips over, shoots to my throat. It practically collides with my pounding heart.

Before I can think about what that means, the voice of the woman onstage speaks again. "When I start singing, it all shifts." Her laughter is husky.

The guitar player appears wearing a leather jacket, even on this sweltering London night. Then the bass player, a cellist, and the drummer file onto the stage.

"Thank you all for coming out to see The Loop. They're our good friends and we owe it to them for inviting us. I would've been happy to stand in the audience with you." She laughs again. "But they insisted we play despite my unrelenting stage fright."

Someone cheers encouragement.

Her eyes dart around as though she's trying to see past the

darkness and into the faces of the crowd. "Are any of you afraid of something?"

There's whistling and a chorus of people shouting variations of the affirmative and one deep baritone answers with a *no.* A few people laugh.

Am I afraid of anything? Yes, the way I feel about Antonio. The way he makes me feel...free. Am I ready to let the grief subside? I won't forget Marcus, but can I move on? I'm afraid to let go of the familiar for what could be...

She continues. "I don't think we talk about our fears enough. We probably think about them plenty. I know I do. What I mean to say is I don't think we talk about our not-fears enough. The things that light us up. For me, it's singing. So there I was, eighteen, terrified of speaking in public, but loved to sing. I was in my brother's band and they wanted to do shows. I refused. So unbeknownst to me, they recorded one of our practices, set up a gig, invited me to it, and then aired the video of the practice at the club. I was mortified, mostly, but watching that girl projected up there, the crowd went crazy. They loved it. Then, as you can imagine, they insisted I get up on stage and sing live. I couldn't say no even though I was shaking." She holds up her hand to demonstrate it's true even now.

The only thing keeping my hand from doing the same is Antonio's grip on it. But my inner shakiness is because of him. When people think of butterflies, they imagine the flutter of delicate wings. These things in my belly beat their warrior wings with the force of a hurricane or a DC-10 plane—my father is a pilot.

"They were so excited, and the truth is, I wanted to sing, just not in front of people. So I tricked myself into thinking it was just my brother and his two friends who'd known me since I was in diapers." She lets out more husky laughter. "So I did it. There was a moment; it was as though time stopped when I could see everyone's beautiful face, the pain, the joy, the *them*ness. I decided from there on out, I had to sing despite my fear. So I started to think of fear as a gift. That sounds wacky, but it's true.

Not the bear mauling you in the woods kind of fear. The fear I'm talking about is the kind you feel when you're on the edge of something huge, transformative. It tells us to get out there and play big. So that's my story. And what I want your story to be—whatever your not-fears are, do that thing that lights you up, despite fears and obstacles. You owe it to your audience, whoever they are."

I feel something big, transformative, and life-changing. He's standing right next to me, holding my hand.

The guitar cranks, the cymbal rattles, and the cello slices one smooth note through the room. The singing begins, and I don't doubt that every single person here transcends time and space and thoughts and fears.

Antonio and I dance to the faster-paced songs. To the slower ones, we sway, our arms brushing, our skin pressing together, and at the end, when the lights turn down and the only sound is the soft chatter of the spellbound audience, he leans in and says, "That was amazing."

I agree, but all I feel is Antonio's proximity. The feel of his breath on the skin behind my ear, on my neck, and the clutch of his hand on my shoulder.

We stay and watch the Loop, which has a super high-energy vibe to the first singer's emotional heart. With the rest of the audience, we sing along to the cover songs we know, shouting the lyrics, sweating, jumping, bouncing, and laughing as though our lives depend on it. Maybe they do rely on moments like these. I hope so.

There's no personal space, no separation as our bodies mash together from the movements of the crowd. Antonio glances at me when they play an encore and everyone's going mad and singing. The look fills me, makes me feel all glowy. I've never felt something like this before. All I know is that I like it. A lot.

After their set, we wander to the quieter part of the club by the bookshelf. Antonio returns with cold drinks. I slurp the fizzy beverage through a straw and taste almonds.

I glance at the framed photos on the wall and then at Antonio's hand. I look up at the wall again, doing a double take that almost results in a spit-take.

The label next to a photograph of a palm pressing against a mirror with a familiar reflection in the background identifies the photographer as *Antonio Moretti*. My jaw drops.

His lips quirk.

"Is there something I don't know?" I ask.

"A lot of things, probably."

Similar black and white works of photographic art cover the walls. How did I not notice these when we were here before? Oh, right. Because I was busy looking at the artist. "You're a photographer?"

His nod is boyish, slightly shy. "My life is art. It's a love letter..."

My heart stutters as I wonder if I've read him wrong. Never mind whether I have a boyfriend, does he have a girlfriend? Of course, he must. Multiple. This isn't a chick flick where the cutest, sweetest guy I've ever met happens to be single and interested in me.

I wonder about the girl who he writes his love letters to. What would it feel like to receive that kind of adoration and affection?

Then I tell myself he's a Romeo, not boyfriend or husband material. I'm not looking, anyway. Not for a boyfriend, husband, or any kind of -nd, whatever else there may be.

"...To you," he says, answering the question I didn't and couldn't ask. The reply is so simple, so earnest that my heart thump, thump, thumps to the jaunty bass line playing over the speakers. Then he adds, "It's a love letter to everyone including myself."

Oh. So maybe no girlfriend?

"*Andiamo,*" he says, reaching for my hand.

We wind through the crowd, pausing every few paces when someone greets Antonio, him kissing them on each cheek and chatting for a moment as though they've reunited after not seeing each other for years. I gather it's merely been days or hours.

Antonio pushes through a door that says *Employees Only* and into a dank hall with exposed plumbing. Signs and supplies from the cafe stack in heaps and piles.

We enter a room with a sofa, a table set up with food and drinks and the first band, Mega, hanging out. The singer, backlit by a mirror framed in round lights, perches on a square table. She lifts her head belting out her husky laughter.

Without preamble, Antonio strides over and in the most authentic, friendly, and unassuming way makes introductions. In moments, the three of us, along with her two companions, chat and laugh.

What she said about fear comes to mind. Courage steps up. Like a duel in an old west town, the two face off.

Fear: of looking at the growing feelings I have for Antonio. For what that could mean about my love for Marcus.

Courage: to do it because all we have is now. Because I've already lost love once.

Which will win?

CHAPTER 12
ALL THE WORLD IS (BACK) STAGE
ANTONIO

Colette and I talk to Misha, the woman from the band Mega, and her friends about their travels and where ours may take us.

When Izzy calls them over to pay their cut of the night's take, Colette gives me an uncertain smile. It echoes my uncertainty. Where do we stand? What is this?

What Misha said about fear springs to mind. I tell it to take a back seat. I feel an internal vibration, like something inside me shifts and then wakes up.

This would be the scene in the musical, where we duet.

I twirl Colette around so we both face the mirror.

"This is us," I whisper.

"What are we?" she asks.

"Courageous."

She blinks a few times at our reflections then turns, stunning me with her dark brown eyes. "The roots of the word *courage* have to do with the heart. It used to mean, 'To speak one's mind by telling by telling all one's heart.'"

"And what does your heart say?" I lean closer.

"I don't think we're all that different—we've both been seeking. I think we've found what we're looking for." Her tone is low, a secret between us.

I smile at her boldness. At her beauty.

She looks up at me through from under her long lashes. Her lips part slightly.

My breath catches. My surroundings turn fuzzy, practically disappear.

Then someone carrying a bulky piece of music equipment knocks into me. I lurch into Colette, and like dominos, we start to fall. I manage to get my footing and reach out for her, but she tips backward, out of reach, and...into a trash can.

I scramble to help her out.

Where I expect to see her wearing a dumbfounded or concerned expression, she bursts into laughter. I take her hands, helping her like by the fountain. No sooner is she on her feet than someone grips my shoulder, turning me around.

A woman wearing a short gray skirt and halter-top lifts onto tiptoes and moves to kiss me. I turn my head in Colette's direction, dodging the other woman.

"I haven't seen you in ages," she purrs. I vaguely remember her from another time I saw a band here.

Disappointment washes the rosy flush from Colette's cheeks, from our almost-kiss.

I hover between choices: be courageous or brush off the girl who just inserted herself into my moment with Colette.

There's something tangible, undeniable between us. Against all odds, we've repeatedly run into each other in one of the biggest cities in Europe.

Yet, we've almost kissed a few times now and each time something interrupted us. Well, except that time under the bridge, but does that count? The fact that I've thought about it every day since it happened suggests that it does. But I want more. I want a real kiss. Not a surprise or speedy kiss. One that lingers and lasts.

"I choose courage," I blurt. I'll tell her and anyone who asks how I feel.

The space between Colette's eyebrows pinches together.

"Hi. This is Colette, my girlfriend," I say, introducing her to the girl in the halter-top.

Her gaze darts to Colette's hand. "I see how it is."

Then I remember that she's a widow. That she's completing the bucket list she made with her high school sweetheart. She told me she doesn't have a boyfriend, but I worry her heart still belongs to someone else. Someone I'll never be.

The ember within dims.

"Girlfriend," Colette repeats.

"Well, if you change your mind, you have my number." The woman in the halter-top wiggles her fingers in a wave as she side-eyes Colette. "You have some garbage—" She points to her arm. Then to me, she says, "I remember you mentioning you like my perfume."

I won't deny that I've dated plenty, but I don't play games.

"But I don't remember your name," I mutter then turn to Colette. "Are you okay?"

"I was." Her eyes search me. "What was that?"

"Seriously, I don't remember her name. We met here a while ago. Hung out a bit. That was it."

"No, I mean the girlfriend thing." The way she says it makes me feel like I went head first into the trash can.

"The girlfriend thing?" I repeat.

"Why'd you say that?" Her voice trembles.

"Because I thought—" Unable to read her expression, I shake my head. I can't pretend we're anything other than friends. Two people on an adventure. To expect something more is too much. "I'm sorry," I say instead.

I have a moment of anticipation, an eagerness for her to say something like, *But I'm not sorry. I want to be your girlfriend.*

She plucks a straw wrapper from her elbow and grimaces. "I should go back to my hotel. Shower and change. I feel gross."

It's easy enough to read between the lines. She still has feelings for Marcus, her high school sweetheart. It breaks my heart that I intruded, practically trampled on her emotions and made her feel gross. Well, it's not entirely my fault the girl recognized me. I dismiss the mixed signals she's sent and the longing of my heart.

We walk back toward her hotel, passing clubs and restaurants still open at this late hour. From a market, the scent of frying sausage and chips scents the air.

I don't want tonight to end. "Can we make one more stop?" I ask.

"As long as you don't let me fall into any garbage cans, sure. What were the odds?"

I fight a smile. I've been asking that exact question, but about us—probably a dumb thing to do.

Under canopies lined with glowing ambient light, people line up for snacks, and squeeze into picnic tables and an assortment of seating arrangements. Colette reaches for my hand, probably so she doesn't lose me in the crowd. At least, that's what I tell myself so I don't get excited again.

Squished between a kabob stall and a tent selling fresh-squeezed lemonade, a woman wearing a yellow baseball hat fills colorful little cups with gelato in a dwindling line.

"Antonio," she calls, smiling. "What brings you here tonight? Oh, right, you know that Samantha has the best gelato in town." There's no denying the flirtation in her voice.

Colette seems to shrink, like she wants to fade into the night.

Izzy.

The woman at the club.

Now, Samantha.

I suddenly realize exactly how this must look to Colette, confirming her accusation that I'm a stereotypical Romeo. But I'm not. Right? I wince.

"That guy that kept coming around for free samples of lemon gelato is back. Remember him?" Samantha asks.

"Of course," I say around laughter at the memory. I nudge Colette's arm with my elbow. "He would dress up as Harry Potter and wave a wand, demanding a sample."

Samantha nods, giving someone change. "He's around here somewhere, you've been warned."

"No doubt he wants to curse me after I shut him off. No more free samples."

"What can I get for you?" Samantha asks me as she eyes Colette.

I feel protective and wish I was the one who put that ring on her finger to signify she's mine and I'm hers—off the market. However, this time I don't dare introduce her as my girlfriend.

"I'll take the chocolate espresso. Do you want a scoop?" I ask Colette.

Before she answers, Samantha bats her eyelashes at me. "You were always such an Italian."

Yeah, a real Romeo. Okay. I get it. Time to clean up my act.

I don't dare look at Colette's expression. Her voice is wooden when she says, "I've never had gelato."

"Then I insist you try every kind like when you couldn't decide what kind of cookie to get earlier."

"We only feature six flavors at a time." Samantha serves an extra-large cup to me even though I only wanted a small scoop.

Colette's eyes widen. "That's a lot of gelato."

"Antonio has a big appetite." Samantha lifts and lowers her eyebrows.

"No. I'm not hungry." Colette's voice hardens.

"You don't have to be hungry for gelato," I say.

"I'll wait for the real thing when I visit Italy someday."

"This is the real thing. Imported," Samantha says sharply.

Colette wraps her arms around her chest as if she's cold and gazes at a stall with crocheted blankets.

"I guess that'll be all." I pull out my wallet and pass Samantha a few bills.

She waves me off. "Your money is no good here."

I stuff the money into the tip jar. "*Grazie*."

With a half-smile in goodbye, I direct Colette away from the crowd and sit on a low wall.

Around a bite of the gelato, I say, "I can't believe you've never tried this."

"How can you eat ice cream with such a tiny spoon?"

I use the small utensil to point at the chocolate espresso. "This is not ice cream."

"Potatoes, poh-tah-toes. Same difference."

"Not even close. That's like saying a Fiat and a Ferrari are the same." The former parks in a slim spot across the road. "You haven't lived until you've tasted gelato."

Colette presses her lips together as if she's resisting but close to giving in.

"Would it help I told you that my first job in London was at that gelato stand? I met Samantha because she was having a hard time understanding her distributor. I translated. Took a job when she offered." Not that I need to work for tips. My resources are vast.

"How long have you been here?"

"I came to London several years ago. I liked it, so I had to figure out a way to support my habit."

"What's your habit?" Alarm rings in her voice.

I chuckle. "Writing love letters."

"Is that an expensive habit?"

"It's worth every penny, and the jobs helped improve my English. I started out making too many mistakes when speaking so I had to nip that in the butt."

She cracks a smile. "It's nip it in the *bud*."

I shift closer as the tension between us eases. "I know."

Her eyes narrow in playful suspicion. "You've known every time, haven't you?"

I hold up my hands in surrender. "I plead the fifty."

She cringes. "You mean you plead the fifth? That one didn't

really work...and I don't think they have the same constitution here in England."

We both have laughter in our voices.

"Are you sure you don't want a taste?" I ask, holding out the spoon.

She bites the inside of her lip then takes the bite. Her eyes flutter close. "Wow," she breathes. "Delicious."

All I can think about is kissing her again and meaning it this time. I lean in, ready to taste the chocolate on her lips when her eyes blink open. She smiles then takes the gelato cup from my hand. She can have all of it, all of me. If she wants.

"Does this flavor have a name?"

"*Bacio,*" I reply. "It means kiss. This is when life kisses you. A big chocolaty kiss. This is how you live life like a love letter."

"What if you want to kiss it back?" she asks, breathy.

"Then you must go slow, savor it the Italian way."

She draws back and looks at the Fiat. I remember her comment about fast Italian sports cars. But I didn't mean I want to take it slow. I meant for us to linger in the kiss. To enjoy it. Not to rush or have anyone interrupt, interfere.

A rowdy group of teens passes, a dog barks, someone sings a Beatles song, and it echoes in the nearby alley. The moment is lost.

The problem is, I'm afraid we won't have another one.

CHAPTER 13
SPEEDBUMPS
COLETTE

Oh, what a night. You'd think I'd have collapsed into bed once I got back to my hotel after the long day—theater, fish and chips, the bookstore, Antonio...and more Antonio. There's so much Antonio.

The sun-kissed skin. His messy curls. And his hands. It's been so long since I've felt a connection like this. It's physical but somehow deeper too. Like something tethers us together. But who wouldn't be attracted to a guy like him? Half the city is smitten, but we'll get to that.

Back to the man's hands.

Every chance I get, I study them like a sculptor, like I'm the photographer learning about motion, angles, light—the musculature, the nail beds, the rough side of his palms. The second I saw the photo on the wall at the AV Club, I knew they belonged to him.

How could hands that perfect belong to anyone else?

Why didn't he tell me about his photography?

What is this giddiness inside?

Our paths have repeatedly crossed and have been drawn together against the odds. However, it isn't lost on me that we've also had multiple opportunities to kiss and missed them.

"So what is it? God? Fate? Cupid? I'm not sure who's in charge of this particular matter, but do you want us to be...or not to be?" I mutter into the dark.

Earlier, after Antonio walked me back to the hotel, we did the awkward little *are-we-going-to-kiss?* dance. He bopped forward. I dipped to the right. He moved in. I shimmied to the other side.

Then I hit a speedbump. Several, in fact.

I'm not ready.

We settled on a hug. He may as well have patted me on the head and said, *Well, you didn't make a complete fool of yourself.*

But I did, folks.

I fell into a trash can.

Did you get that? Is there anything remotely less attractive than tipping backward and folding in half into a round bin filled with empty cups, food remnants, used napkins, and who knows what else?

But I'm not going to lie. The hug felt good. Like chocolate gelato good. Why hadn't I ever tried it before? Oh, right because Marcus once told me I wouldn't like it—too milky. He was more of a ribs and bacon kind of guy.

All this time, I've believed myself to be a cookie-girl, but maybe I'm a gelato-girl.

I had no idea what I was missing with that creamy, lush, rich, and chocolaty frozen deliciousness.

The gelato and the Antonio hug left me wanting more...and wondering.

I was exhausted before, but it's like I took a shot of espresso on the elevator up to my room.

Marcus was wonderful. I've gathered up all my memories of him, packaged them in shiny paper and ribbons, and set them and him up on a pedestal.

He was the best high school sweetheart a girl could ask for. A best friend.

But he wasn't perfect. Not like Antonio's hands.

Or his hair.

His smile.

His laugh.

My sigh is so loud it probably alarmed the dog that barks outside.

No. Antonio isn't perfect either.

No one is. Marcus included. Yet, I've been comparing everyone I've ever dated to him. There was the time he ran over a squirrel and kept going. I know, awful. Then he got rowdy at a party once and mooned everyone. Even though he was an athlete, it wasn't a pretty sight. He forgot my birthday once and tried to make up for it by saying it was his grandparents' fiftieth wedding anniversary and he was busy planning a party with his sisters. Grandad Larsen had passed four years prior.

But he was good in so many ways that those things didn't matter. They still don't, but I haven't allowed room for anyone else to make mistakes or expect them to be anything less than perfect.

After losing Marcus, I wanted the opposite of emptiness, solitude, and loneliness. I wanted the antonyms, words to fill in the gaps, to fill me. But I realize it's a bridge that I have to build, that I am building out of places, people, new friends, foods, conversations had, tears shed, laughter shared. I'm building it piece by piece, out of parts of this journey.

Antonio included.

At least I'd like for him to be.

But there's a big *but*. And I don't mean the *nip it in the butt* kind of butt. I've succumbed to his smolder and I'm not the only one. He called me his *girlfriend* then pulled back. It seemed like he instantly regretted it. Maybe the word slipped out of his mouth and he meant to introduce me to the girl wearing little more than a handkerchief as his "former" girlfriend. Note: Grandmama and Mama never would have let me out of the house dressed like that. They always said it was better to leave a lot to the imagination.

That makes me think about what Antonio said about anticipation. Well, buddy, you've got me wound up for a kiss real good.

But back to the girlfriend thing. When I heard that word, something pulsed in me and wanted to shout, *Yes!* from the rooftops.

But maybe he meant to say garbage girl instead of girlfriend.

I mull this over as the hours tick by. I think he's slightly nocturnal. Hazel has said Europeans tend to keep later hours. For instance, in Spain, it's not uncommon to eat dinner at ten or eleven p.m. Are cultural practices contagious because being out with him at night makes me feel so free. Like anything could happen. Like we have the world at our fingertips. Adventure, magic, kisses...

Or perhaps I have reverse jet lag. Is there such a thing?

I drift in my thoughts until the fringed night gives way to gentle morning light, sending a hush over me and I finally fall asleep.

In the next days, Antonio and I traipse across the city in the rain, in the sunshine, and on days when the weather doesn't know what to do and neither do I.

I've crossed everything off the bucket list for London, including the London Eye Ferris wheel, the British Museum, National Gallery, Westminster Abbey, Saint Paul's Cathedral, and standing in the eastern and western hemispheres on the Prime Meridian in Greenwich.

But I'm not sure about what's next. I'm supposed to leave for Amsterdam in two days. I've spent a week with Antonio. It feels like seven years, not seven days. We've teased the idea of him joining me, but so far no commitment.

I haven't been explicit in my plans, and he hasn't asked.

The obvious thing to do would be to talk about it like two rational adults. But there's nothing rational about the way I feel about him. Or how the concept of commitment sends a rash of fear through me. So what do I do?

I blame it on a language barrier. He wouldn't understand my

trepidation, my healing heart, and my confusion—even if I tried to explain. How do I know that? Because I don't quite understand it myself. That's a good enough excuse for me.

We've visited stores and parks, galleries, and pubs. Sought entertainment, diversion, amusement.

I exist in a state that swings between avoidance and fervid excitement—like I'm sixteen all over again. I don't want to go to sleep at night because I'm afraid I'll miss something but can't bear to wake up in the morning. It's as though my mind is in neutral and my body is in near-constant motion, covering miles of sidewalk, of cobblestones, of time.

But each step brings me closer to departure.

We're passing through Piccadilly and the Eros fountain where Antonio and I first met.

"Want a doughnut?" he asks.

I recall the love list the girls made me, tucked somewhere in my bag. "I'd like to toss a coin in the fountain and make a wish."

He tells me about the Trevi fountain in Italy. "If you toss a coin over your right shoulder and make a wish, it's said it'll come true."

"Have you tried it?"

"Yes. Instead, I hit a tourist in the head with my coin. I quickly tried again and wished he didn't come after me." He chuckles.

I laugh. "What about Eros? Does he grant wishes?"

"Wishes we didn't know we had." His eyes drift to mine.

Does everything out of his mouth have to sound like poetry? Not that I'm complaining, but I'm teetering on the edge here.

My pulse picks up. "What was the wish?"

"A love letter kind of life."

"Are you done writing it?" I foolishly and dangerously want nothing more than for the love letter he talks about to be addressed to me.

He shakes his head. "They're never done. Not really."

The clouds knock invisibly into each other in the sky, crowding the sun in an effort to make the day gloomy.

But with Antonio, it isn't. It would be impossible for clouds, rain, potential girlfriends, or anything to turn off his smile.

But my mouth dips. Saying goodbye soon might change that.

I make my wish, toss the coin, and wait for it to plop into the water. Instead, it bounces off the side and into the gutter. I wilt.

"Want to try again?" Antonio asks, digging into his pockets.

But neither one of us has another coin.

"I'm dog-sitting tonight," he announces. "I should head over there soon."

I raise my eyebrows in question. "This is news."

"Friends of mine are out of town for the weekend and I'm on duty until dawn. The gig includes a fancy kitchen and money to buy ingredients for dinner. I wasn't done wowing you with my culinary skills."

"You live many lives, Mr. Moretti," I say.

He holds out his hand for me to take—I accept the wordless invitation to join him.

"Nope. Just the one life," he says.

"The love letter one?"

He winks.

This man might be my undoing. How is it fair he can get away with being so flirty, so spontaneous, so gelato-delicious looking?

It's cooler with the overcast sky, but it may as well be a sweltering day in the desert. I practically melt right there on the sidewalk. That man should register his eyes, his lips, and the way he combines the two in a smolder as lethal weapons.

Wide-eyed, I follow him like a silly puppy.

At a modern flat in Shoreditch, Antonio opens the door and a bulldog waddles out, licks him, sniffs me, and then stands at the door, tossing us a *hurry-up* look.

We take Ralph for a walk as the sun, making a final appearance, bathes the charcoal, tan, and russet buildings in golden light.

"Hungry?" Antonio asks.

My stomach tosses with hunger and anxiety about my next steps to complete the bucket list.

Antonio speaks a string of Italian. The words loop and curve romantically until I realize he's talking about food, dishes he could make for dinner.

"Tortellini?" I say, hoping I accurately picked up on something he said.

"*Sorpresa.*" Then he adds, "Surprise."

We stop at a market where Ralph noses baskets of truffles. Antonio bounds from stall to stall acquiring a paper bag filled with groceries. A loaf of fresh Italian bread pokes out of the top, like in romantic movies set in Europe, giving me a shot of warm fuzzies.

"All we need is a Vespa," I say more to myself than Antonio.

"I had one, well, a Lambretta, another kind of scooter like a Vespa—traded it for a train ticket to Denmark."

A chuckle replaces the warm fuzzies. "Of course you did."

I don't get the sense Antonio is one of those hapless savants like in the previously mentioned movies where he just flows through life from one mishap to good fortune to another. But he has a certain flair, a charm...and I don't think he's a broke backpacker who needs to work as a busboy either.

The thing is, I can't figure this guy out...or my feelings for him.

After washing up in the well-appointed kitchen back at the flat, he puts on an old record. It's a low crooning Italian whose voice transports me back to the movie fantasy. This scene takes place on a terrace on the side of a cliff lit with golden light, bougainvillea, and laughter spilling into the Mediterranean. Under a trellis, there's a large table, covered in food and fresh bread, chatter between young and old, lovers and relatives, new friends and people who've known each other forever. It's home-coming and reunion. It's comfort and happiness. It's a love letter that I hope to write someday.

But would I? Could I write it with this man who hands me a clove of garlic, breaking my imaginative reverie?

"You chop." He whizzes around the kitchen, giving me little jobs until the music changes, a jaunty tune made for dancing. He takes me by the hand, spinning me around.

I try hard not to think about how my fingers smell like garlic.

The ever-present slight lift in his lips, the hint of amusement, turns into a full-on smile when our noses brush as he dips me back. We stay like that, suspended with him supporting my low spine. I grasp his strong shoulders. His hair tickles me and laughter pours forth, like water in the fountain, like it's impossible for there to be sadness in a world like this, in a world where people write love letters with their lives.

This could be it. The kiss. Nothing interrupts us this time.

But he draws an uneven breath, straightens, and returns to the stove.

I can't possibly have garlic breath. We haven't eaten yet. Must be my hands.

Antonio sets the table, lighting a candle and setting out bubbly water for each of us—he says it has gas. *I sure hope not.*

Once settled, he lifts his glass in a toast. "*Salud,*" he says as we clink.

When I sip, it tastes like carbonated water with a hint of lemon.

The dish, a mixture of oregano and garlic, fresh tomato, basil, olives is as good as the gelato, but in a savory way.

A moan escapes. "What kitchen wizardry is this?"

"Puttanesca." Antonio's accent dances over the word. "When I was a kid, I didn't like the capers, but my tastes evolved."

"Capers?"

"The salty peas," he says, holding one out on a fork.

He tells me about learning to cook from his grandmother, Nonna, the kitchens he's worked in across Europe, and the necessity of good food. "You always have to feed the food-heart."

I tilt my head and grin. "The food-heart? Is that an anatomical term? If so, I don't think they teach it in medical school." But I don't really need him to explain. This time with Antonio has nourished me in a way I've never before experienced.

This is only the second meal he's prepared, but I sure could get used to stuffing my food-heart.

"So you'll take the train in the morning," he says. "It's an early departure. Around eight a.m., I think."

"The train. Right." I want to complete the items on the bucket list, but what am I leaving behind? Hazel would tell me that I'm having a serious case of FOMO.

Get your mind out of the gutter. It's not a curse word. It means *Fear Of Missing Out*.

As I look up at this man with messy curls, dark stubble, and lips that look like they could feed my food-heart and then some, a feeling lands in my chest.

When I leave, I know exactly what I'll be missing and it terrifies me.

CHAPTER 14
YO, GO!
ANTONIO

My heart slams against my ribs like a door closing. Traveling with Colette would be a dream come true. I even quit my job. YOLO. *You Only Live Once,* right?

I thought leaving here together was the plan. Women travel alone all the time, but we don't need that turnip truck breaking down in a dodgy part of town, now do we?

But she's guarded, keeps everything bolted and locked up tight. I don't want to overstep any boundaries she has, but that living, beating thing in my chest won't stop knocking.

We talked casually about traveling together during the dinner at my place, but it's never come up since. I want to go with her but am waiting for an invitation even though I know better than to take this further.

Where's my brain when I need it to tell me to keep it down and not get involved?

"It's your last night in the city. There's something I want you to see." I'm about to hold out my hand for her to take but then remember I went too far when I said that she was my girlfriend.

When we were dancing, I felt the spark between us again. Do I ignore it?

It's a back and forth, a push and pull. This is new to me—

with all the other women I've been with, it's full steam ahead until we crash and burn.

Does Colette want distance, space? Nothing like putting a couple of countries between us to achieve that goal. I can't figure her out.

Athena once told me that some American women don't take kindly to chivalry, claiming they want to be independent. They can hold a door open themselves, for instance. I hold open a door for a person because it's the kind thing to do, and it makes me happy to know I can lighten someone's load. It's part of writing a love letter out of my life.

What about Colette? Does she want to do this trip on her own or does she want me along, holding open doors? I think about this while I coax Ralph to the stairwell and gesture for Colette to follow.

We pass the first, second, and third floors. Together, we go through the wide metal door to the roof with a garden containing a patch of strawberries, a tub of tomatoes, and bushels of herbs. Grapevines border it all. I'm reminded of home as I water the plants.

Then we climb onto a platform by the building's chimney. My friends keep outdoor furniture up here for the summer months. We sit side by side on the wicker couch and our legs and arms brush. Ralph settles by our feet.

The city spreads in every direction with the ribbon of the river bordering one side. The horizon disappears with the sunset as lights blink on like little fireflies.

"The first night I was here, I stayed with these friends. Restless and unable to sleep, I came up here." I sweep my hand across the vista.

"It's beautiful."

My gaze turns to Colette and I prepare to tell her a part of my journey I've never shared with anyone. "While my mother was pregnant, she wrote a love letter to her baby. Me." I pause, pained that she wrote how much she already adored me but left, anyway. "That was when I decided to write a love letter to my life. I didn't have to sell gelato, bus tables, and make coffee at a cafe over on Regent Street for a while—espresso is my specialty."

'Then why did you?"

"Because English isn't my first language, I worked at those places to improve my speaking but more to see people in their daily lives. To take away barriers between myself and *amore*." I'm about to tuck my hands away as I realize I've been talking with them, getting more impassioned with each word. "I used to hold back, embarrassed by my how do you say it? *My yes for life*."

"Zest for life." Her eyes sparkle.

I nod. Same thing. "All this time, I thought I was looking for the woman who wrote me that letter, my mother. But I'm not so sure anymore. Maybe this experience was so I could write my own love letter...then figure out who to send it to."

She grips my arm and my breath catches. "Don't say that. Don't give up."

I shake my head. "If I was looking for love…" I turn back to the cityscape so I can't see her expression when I say the next part. "I think I found it."

After a beat, she says, "We should all write more love letters."

"I thought my mother left me in silence, when really what she left me with was so much to say. Words to learn, experiences to have, people to meet. I thought she left me alone, when really what she left me with was an opportunity to get to know myself and to make new friends. I thought she left me wanting and needing. I've tried filling the emptiness when really it was spaciousness, room to fill with yesterday and today and tomorrow." I can no longer resist and angle to see her expression.

"I'm starting to understand what you mean. I've learned so much this past week about myself, life, love."

The sounds filter up from the street below, but my quickened pulse pounds in my ears.

Colette turns to face me.

The spark lights up within.

Her dark, fathomless eyes lift to mine.

Joyful, intense anticipation fills me.

She slides her smooth hand against my rough palm.

My brain and I have a quick word. More of an argument. I win but remain a gentleman and will drive a Fiat if that's what Colette wants. I lift her hand to my lips and kiss it.

Then she nestles against my chest.

I wrap my arms around her like a blanket as we watch the city go to sleep.

After a while, she says, "What language do you dream in?"

I think about this a moment. "Italian, English, nonsense." I chuckle. "Most of my dreams are nonsense."

Except one...and that's to love this woman with all my heart forever.

But I know well enough that not all dreams come true.

She yawns, and that's my signal to make sure she gets back to the hotel safely. Tomorrow is a big travel day. She insists on taking a cab back to the hotel even though I offer to walk her. Likely, she's tired.

When it pulls up, she opens the door, and says, "So every day is a love letter?"

I tip my head forward and back once. "Yes. Every day."

Then she gets in a taxi, and that's it. I stand starkly on the sidewalk until the taillights disappear, fearing I won't see the love of my life ever again.

But something in my mother's journal comes to mind about letting things go—I think it was something like, "If you let something go and it comes back, it's yours forever. If not, it was never meant to be."

Sleeping is futile, so I get Ralph and his leash. We wander along the quiet streets, and I don't mind that the dog has to stop every few steps to sniff. Maybe he's writing his own love letter to the scent of other dogs, trash, and shrubs.

I shiver under the cloud cover. As if on cue, the sky splits open, releasing plump drops of rain. Ralph protests and we hightail it back to the flat.

Hoping Colette will materialize, I glance down the street, but it's empty...and that's just how I feel.

I hardly sleep and am startled when a key turns in the lock near dawn. Ralph barks. The door swings open and Stefano and Cleo enter, arguing in Italian.

With one look at me, they go quiet.

"What's the matter?" Stefano frowns. "You look like the night chewed you up and spit you out."

I brush my hand through my hair. "That bad?"

Cleo wags her finger at me. "It's about a woman. I know that look. Who was it this time?"

Despite what Colette assumed about me being a Romeo, I've had my heart broken more than once.

"What's her name? Give us details." Cleo is a petite woman with shiny black hair tied in a low ponytail but speaks with the authority of a general.

Stefano adds, "Our flight was changed, so we came back early. Missed this guy." He fusses over Ralph.

Cleo doesn't let me off the hook though and I give them the abbreviated story of meeting Colette.

"She's getting on a train to Amsterdam in an hour?" Cleo speaks as if we don't speak the same language.

"What are you doing here?" Stefano asks as he prepares espresso and then passes me a cup.

I down it in one sip. "House sitting." I point to Ralph.

Cleo brushes her hand dismissively then shoos me toward the door. "You have to go."

I tuck my head back. "What?"

"Go after her. Get on that train," Stefano orders me.

I shift from foot to foot. "It's crossed my mind."

Cleo levels me with an arched-eyebrow glare that only an Italian woman can deliver. "Are you scared?"

I scratch the back of my head and then nod because no way will they let me get away with denying it.

"Then you should do it," Stefano says.

"Definitely," Cleo adds. Then, linking her arm through her husband's, they smile. "That's one thing we agree on."

"Interesting logic." I should be counseling them on their love life, but they gather up my overnight bag, stuffing random things in it, including a book that isn't mine. Before I can say as much, Cleo thrusts the bag in my arms.

"Go. You're no longer welcome here. Not even if you miss the train. Take the next one." She wears a fierce smile so I know she's doesn't hate me. Neither is she messing around.

Excitement and fear slice through me. "You think I should do it?"

Ralph barks as if in agreement.

Then Cleo wraps her arms around me in a hug before shoving me out the door. "Ciao," she calls.

I race down the street, keeping pace with a cab and flailing my arms until it stops. "St. Pancras station, please."

"You're in a hurry, mate? I can't promise you won't miss your train."

"No, I don't want to miss a girl."

He chuckles as if understanding my urgency and peels into traffic.

Although I've never driven a car in London, I know the roads and routes well enough along with traffic patterns. When we're still four blocks away, my leg jitters.

I still have forty-seven minutes, but I have to get a ticket and check in thirty minutes before the train departs. Then I have to find Colette.

When we're still a couple of blocks away, I can no longer take it. I thrust a wad of bills into the front, giving the cabbie a sizable tip, and rush down the sidewalk, shouting, "YOLO!" like I'm running from the police officer who found us under the bridge.

Sprinting to the station, I dodge a school field trip and a

coffee cart. I vault over a child's wagon filled with soccer balls. I'm nearly there, feeling home free, when a group of tourists shuffles by the main doors, blocking me. I elbow my way through, feeling the clock ticking along with my pulse.

The line for tickets is long and I bob between two, trying to gauge the shorter one. Sweat beads my hairline. Announcements call over the speakers, indicating departures.

I'm about to book my ticket, but it's too late. The computerized reservation system clocked out purchases with a red error message. My shoulders drop.

"Hey, mate. You done?" asks the guy in line behind me.

No, I'm not done. But maybe fate is. Perhaps I wasn't meant to go after Colette.

I scan the crowd as travelers and locals stride past, some meandering and others with purposeful strides. Not one of them is a petite woman with a shock of blond hair and the prettiest eyes I've ever seen.

Someone taps my shoulder. I turn slowly. Colette stands there with her luggage in one hand and a pair of tickets in the other.

"*Andiamo*?" she asks.

CHAPTER 15
BETRAYED BY A ROBOT
COLETTE

Antonio's smile can only be described as the sunrise. The corners of his lips lift slowly as if he's on top of the world.

"I was hoping you'd get here in time," I say.

"But how'd you know I was coming?"

"I guess I didn't, but I thought—never mind." I skip the part that makes me feel vulnerable like a baby bird. Instead, I go for the whimsical. "I had a dream about a handsome Italian guy and a bunch of other nonsense." True story.

His eyebrows twitch quizzically.

"He was speaking Italian to me, but I couldn't understand. I replied in English. He didn't understand." Then he kissed me on the lips. That part I understood...and didn't want to wake up, but I don't reveal that part. I dreamt of Antonio holding my hand but not leading me. Rather, walking by my side.

"Will you keep me from falling off the turnip truck?" I ask, offering him the extra ticket.

He bundles me in his arms, lifting me off my feet in the biggest, tightest hug ever—it squeezes the heaviness out of me, so I leave it there in an invisible puddle on the ground. Relief sweeps through me.

He leans back and like last night, just before he kissed my hand, our gazes catch. His eyes are like a shot of caffeine, enough to keep me awake for days. I'm hooked, addicted.

The last call announcement for the Eurostar to Amsterdam sounds over the speakers.

Energized, exhilarated, or just crazy about this guy, I grab his hand and we rush through the terminal.

Antonio helps an elderly woman with three small dogs board the train. After getting them settled in, he tells me all about Mini, Bitty, and Baby. "She even showed me photos of them during their visit to London, including Buckingham Palace."

I giggle.

"It was nice of you to help her. She seemed like one of those fussy, dog people. I've always wanted a dog but promised I wouldn't turn into a fanatical Fur-Baby-Mom. You know, the kind that puts their animal in a bag and totes it around. Dresses it in clothes."

He chuckles. "I don't know. It's kind of cute." He winks.

Maybe it's a European thing? Then again, there's plenty of that in America too. I wonder if I'd like a Yorkie.

After traveling along the Thames the countryside spreads in every direction before we dive under the Channel Tunnel.

Antonio and I are relatively quiet as if neither one of us can quite believe this is happening. After a couple of announcements, the smooth hum of the train rocks him to sleep.

I also drift but don't dream. When I wake up, I blink a few times to find Antonio still by my side, wearing a pair of glasses and reading a book in Italian.

This is new.

There's well dressed, swarthy Antonio. *Mama says meow.*

Now, there's foxy, studious Antonio. *I practically purr.*

The only thing that could make this moment better is if he read aloud to me. "Be still my heart," I mutter.

He tilts his head in question. "Did you have a good sleep?"

I yawn and nod. "What are you reading?"

He flashes me the cover of what looks like a book of poetry. "Cleo shoved this in my bag."

I swallow thickly, afraid after I left last night he spent it with another woman. Then I recall a piece of mail on the counter at the flat. *Cleo Denetso.*

"She and Stefano were back early. They were fighting and then practically kicked me out this morning."

"Yikes," I say.

"They insisted I follow you."

I open and close my mouth, fighting with the question I have to ask. "Did you want to come though?"

His calloused hand wraps around mine. "I wouldn't be here if I didn't."

That's exactly what I wanted to hear, but it also makes me feel like I'm standing on top of the moving train instead of safely inside. "Good thing I got you the ticket then."

I need a distraction and fumble for the lowest hanging fruit, knowing I already sound like an idiot before the words are out of my mouth. "Books are great. Poetry too. Do you like to read?"

He nods as if I'd asked, *Do you like gelato?* "Would you rather read on the beach or in a cozy nook by a wood fire?"

"I'm a cozy nook kind of girl." I pick up on the game of would-you-rather. "Would you rather watch the movie or read the book first?"

"Book, always. Would you rather read in your head or out loud?"

"In my head. You?"

He holds up his book of love letters. "Can I read to you?"

"Right now?" I ask, looking around. But no one else sits in our section.

He smirks with his love letter lips, food-heart lips, anticipation lips, Italian lips, kissable lips and then parts the pages of the book. In his accented voice, he reads me the first poem—the story of a woman separated from her lover for twenty years, two continents, and a stolen diamond.

And that is how I fall in love with Antonio's voice. With poetry. With the soft press of his lips when he pauses between passages. With the way the ends of his hair curl. The slope of his nose. His expensive cologne and comfort scent.

When he goes quiet, I ask, "You said you've been to Amsterdam before?"

In the amount of time it takes him to tell me about how he visited friends who'd lost and found love in the city, the landscape changes from fields and farm equipment dotting the horizon, to enormous office buildings and headquarters filling in the gaps in my view.

"I was staying at their place for a little while. Unfortunately, I caught her cheating on him with an Italian guy. I don't hold it against her. He was very handsome."

My stomach sinks. *An Italian guy?*

"It wasn't me if you were wondering. And I'm joking about not holding it against her. I do not approve of breaking that kind of trust. But you can imagine how awkward it was. Needless to say, I found another place to stay."

My exhale is long as his explanation catches up with me.

"Why did you put Amsterdam on your bucket list?" he asks.

"I didn't. Marcus heard it was cool. My additions to the list were London, Paris, and Rome, but I never got around to adding the last one."

The train deposits us in the oldest part of the city and we emerge by a bridge leading over a canal. Like books on a shelf, the buildings stack side by side, spine to spine, each with a unique story to tell. The salty smell of fish and pungent fried onions hits me in the nose.

Antonio buys us a herring sandwich from a stall, insisting it's good for my memory. "Or, making new ones."

I take a couple of bites, wrinkle my nose, and let him finish it.

We spend the morning pottering along the canals, Antonio pointing out historical buildings and recounting stories from his time here. We wander under the shady trees, debating over which of the funky houseboats we'd occupy. It's laughter and ease being with him.

We reach the floating floral market, the *Bloemenmarkt,* where the fresh scent of tulips, the earthen scent of geraniums, and the peonies lure me inside the glass walls.

"I haven't seen you smile like this before," Antonio says.

"Like what?" I ask, my cheeks turning pink.

"Like you're in love."

"Maybe you're rubbing off on me," I say, nudging his hip with mine.

"I hope so."

We meander back toward the station, stopping in art galleries and shops. As twilight descends, we stop in front of a place called *Pannenkoeken* with a narrow blue awning.

"Let's have breakfast," Antonio says.

"But it's dinnertime." I'm not sure anything could top last night's puttanesca. My heart-stomach is still full.

"My friend Femke used to work here." He peers through the window.

He asks after Femke, but she's not here. After an exchange in Dutch with lots of hand gestures, Antonio embraces the young man behind the counter. He introduces me. "Colette, meet Femke's boyfriend, Hendrik. He phoned her and she's on her way."

"My friends call me Hennie," he says in perfect English, telling us about how he and Femke met in London. "Serendipity," he says when we make the connection of our meeting in the same city.

He leaves us seated at a small table by the window and puts our order in. After a coffee refill and more discussion about London, Amsterdam, and various points in between, two orders of thin pancakes appear in front of us. Apples and powdered sugar cover one. The other has a few flakes of smoked salmon and white sauce on top.

Femke appears with bobbed hair and a bright smile. She and

Antonio swap hugs and double kisses on the cheeks. They catch up, reminiscing, trading traveling stories, and asking about people they knew in common.

"But what happened to you? One day you were gone," Femke says. "Poof." She snaps her fingers.

Antonio's shoulder lifts and lowers. "It was time for me to leave."

"Why? Where did you go? I was so worried."

Antonio settles back in his chair. "One day, I was sitting next to the canal and a boat floated by with a woman on the deck, lounging under the sun. Her husband looked upon her, admired her. It was such a *look*. I'll never forget it. It was intense and passionate, caring and gentle. It was as though he would love her even if she jumped out of the boat and swam away. It was a love letter in the eyes. It was beautiful. I wanted to make that feeling my life."

His eyes float to me.

They say more than words ever could.

Warmth fills me.

My breath turns shallow.

I could melt under that sunshiny day that Antonio described and I wouldn't swim away.

He excuses himself to the bathroom and Femke asks, "Have you been together long?"

I stutter, not quite sure we're *together*. "We met a little over a week ago and then every day since...it seems."

Her head inclines in an invitation to explain.

I tell a perfect stranger about how I went to London with little more than a bucket list and on that first day, eating a doughnut in front of a fountain, he saved me from falling in. In many ways, he's saved me from clinging to the past. Then I tell her about each of our encounters from there.

Several cyclists stream by, reminding me how far I am from home, from who I was...and how much I miss my friends.

"I'm not sure we're together though," I say, remembering Marcus and the bucket list.

"But the way he looked at you. Didn't you feel it?" Her smile is intent, genuine.

"But I'm not sure—"

"I don't think it matters because here you are." Her lips catch a smug, knowing smile. "And who wouldn't want to tame that Italian stallion—that's what the girls around here called him." She winks.

I'm about to explain that I'm confused about how I feel and am wary because of the plentitude of women and the Italian stallion status. But Antonio slides back into his seat.

Did he hear us? He meets my blush with an amused smile that makes his eyes sparkle.

"Where are you going next?" Femke asks.

"Everywhere," Antonio answers as though in love with all of these detours, people, and experiences.

Me too.

Perhaps it's the twilight hanging in the air, the fluidity of the canals striping the city, or the proximity of possibility, but the urgency to complete the bucket list dissolves a little. It brought me here, but where I go next doesn't matter as much.

This is an adventure.

We spend the next couple of days touring the city, visiting museums, and strolling along the canals. I consult the itinerary Hazel and Maxwell made for me and reference the bucket list. Yes, I want to see all of these places, especially Paris, but maybe it's time to ditch the map and see where the journey takes me.

Then it's like Marcus calls to me from across the ocean. My eyes mist as though offering to add to all that saltwater. The ache of missing him takes hold, squeezing my chest.

Antonio lounges in the sun beside me. His blue T-shirt would be so easy to drown in too.

Or maybe I'm going about this all wrong. Perhaps he's a raft.

We meet Femke and Hennie for dinner the night before I'm

supposed to go north. Will Antonio come with me or head back to London?

I'm afraid to ask.

However, last night, in my hotel room, I asked Siri a multitude of questions about European men, dating, and if a guy that followed me to a train station wants to be more than friends. Yes, I've seen the movies, but it's different when it's personal. It's me, and I brought my insecurities overseas. Unfortunately, Siri wasn't much help.

We have a long, leisurely meal at an Indian restaurant. It's so spicy, I suggest we get ice cream as they sip their after dinner espressos.

"Not gelato?" Antonio asks.

I don't mention that nothing will compare to the bite he fed me outside the market in London. I'm forever ruined when it comes to gelato...and maybe all things Italian.

Femke tells us about a place that sells frozen yogurt with every conceivable topping—she raves about the fudge, marshmallow, and melty peanut butter sauces. I silently thank her for saving me. Before we leave the restaurant, I excuse myself to the bathroom.

I squat—because even after all this traveling, I'm still not okay with sitting on the seat in a public bathroom—and then hear a plop. No, this isn't an instance of TMI.

I watch as my phone settles on the bottom of the bowl.

Panic seizes me. It was in my back pocket and I forgot to take it out. "No, no, no."

There is no debating. I'm in a foreign country, that device is my lifeline, and there is only one thing to do.

I plunge my hand into the water, thankful I hadn't tinkled yet.

Drying it off with toilet paper is useless because it shreds and little bits stick to the phone case. I've been in here long enough that Antonio probably wonders if I'm okay and that is an image I do not want in his head.

I'm a southern lady for goodness sakes.

I return to the table and try to appear composed and not contaminated. "Sorry that I took so long." My phone beeps and says *I didn't quite get that.* I don't dare tell them what happened because Antonio will never want to hold, no less kiss, my hand again after where it's been.

And you'd better believe I triple washed my hands before leaving that restroom.

The others are talking about a magazine article or something.

The voice from my phone comes again, saying, *Interesting question.*

My stomach knots as I pull out my cell phone and push the buttons, trying to turn it off because that was Siri's exact answer when, last night, I'd asked, *How do I know he loves me*?

Then followed up with, *How do I know I love him*?

Her answer, *I'm not sure how do you know I love him but this is what I found on the web.*

Malfunctioning, the robot lady on my toilet-phone repeats that same response now.

CHAPTER 16
THE VIEW FROM DOWN HERE
ANTONIO

Colette's cheeks turn pink. Her phone repeats *I'm not sure how do you know I love him but this is what I found on the web.*

She fumbles with the buttons.

Again, the smooth robotic voice says *I'm not sure how do you know I love him but this is what I found on the web.*

My lips quirk.

Femke and Hennie incline their heads as though confused.

When the phone says it one more time, Colette tosses the thing like a grenade and then dives beneath the table.

We all exchange an amused look. I peek under the tablecloth. "What are you doing under there?" Laughter and concern lace my voice.

"Hiding."

"From what?"

"You. Technology."

"I'm curious to know what Siri found on the web."

"Dumb articles."

I push out my chair and then crawl under the table to show her the answer. *My answer.* I've asked myself the same question, well, more like, *How do I know she loves me?*

"The answer you're looking for is here." I press her palm to the center of my chest.

"In your pecs?" she asks.

In the low light, I catch the edge of her smile.

"They feel pretty firm."

I laugh. "The heart."

"What about the heart-stomach?"

"There too."

I twine my fingers into hers, kissing the tops of her knuckles. "And here."

"You probably don't want to do that," she says quickly, jerking her hand away.

My face falls.

"I had to fish the phone out of the toilet." She squeezes her eyes shut. "But the water was clean-ish. I washed my hands. I promise. Three times."

"That's what took you so long."

"I forgot the phone was in my back pocket."

"We'll see if we can get it fixed tomorrow." But I'm not entirely convinced it was broken. Maybe it was good Siri spilled her secret searches because now I have a better idea of how she feels.

"Should we go get some frozen yogurt?" I ask.

"Nah. We should stay under here a little longer." Her arms wrap around her knees, tucked up by her chest.

I unwind her arm and kiss the top of her hand again then the inside of her wrist. I plant my lips on the crease of her elbow before landing on her shoulder.

"Colette, if you'll let me, I can do a better job than a robot to tell you how I feel."

Her cheeks go darker and I capture her gaze. The moment is intense, but we'll go slow if that's what she still wants. Gripping her hand, I bring us back to the surface, to the table.

"What other places are on the bucket list?" Femke says.

Colette's voice is slightly shaky when she answers, "Copenhagen and Stockholm. Then Paris."

"Have you been?" Hennie asks me.

I squish up my lips, trying to be modest and nod.

"You've been everywhere." Colette sinks back.

"But not with you."

Famke and Hennie exchange a look like if we weren't so cute they'd be sick.

"The flight is only an hour and a half," I say.

"No, you must travel by train. It's more romantic." Femke giggles.

The next day, Colette cancels her flight and we board a train, first making a quick stop in Osnabruck, Germany then onward to the ICE to Hamburg.

As we watch the landscape slide by, Colette nestles closer to me. In place of so much city brick and concrete, old cathedrals and new high rises, the landscape dawns green: pine and moss, olive and sage. The fields stretch and stretch and stretch in the distance. There is so much space and so much vibrancy. So little in the way of foundations, clear lines of streets, and marked out paths.

I've mostly searched for my mother in the organized chaos of cities, but she could be out there somewhere. But am I still looking? Maybe she'll find me. Where there used to be an empty ache inside, now, there's warmth.

The lullaby motion of the train keeps Colette asleep and her head rests on my shoulder. The excited twinge of her peaceful face so close to mine fills me in a way that confirms my answer to the question she asked her phone.

After a while, a crackly voice sounds over the intercom in multiple languages.

She sits up abruptly.

I stretch and yawn. "We're probably at the *Vogelfluglinie.*"

"The what?"

"The ferry. The train rides the ferry," I explain.

"The train rides the what? How?"

I point out the window at a massive boat, at least four stories tall, occupying the harbor. "The *Vogelfluglinie,*" I repeat. "I've always wanted to ride a train and a boat at the same time."

"A boyhood dream?" she asks.

"No, an adventure," I say with an amused smile, and swing our arms between us as we step outside.

While we wait to board, workers in bright yellow vests swarm the enormous boat, which is a standard ferry with a strange structure surrounding it used to load cars, trucks, and the train for crossing.

I stand close to keep us warm as we get on. Little sparks fizzle on my skin, under my skin, all over and inside.

She quivers and quakes.

"Are you cold? Let's go into the cabin," I suggest.

The buffet in the cafeteria offers fruit and eggs, cheese, toast, and cold meats and fish. Colette and I fill plates. The girl at the register looks up at me in a way that makes me want to have a ring on my finger, a symbol to announce that I'm taken.

"Where are you going?" the girl asks in a flirty voice.

When I glance at Colette's left hand, she's not wearing the ring.

"Did you lose your ring?" I ask.

The girl at the register sighs as if giving up on flirting with me and tallies our items.

We take our food to a vacant table, but Colette picks at her fruit.

I squeeze her fourth finger. "You never answered about the ring."

Her gaze slides to her bare finger. "It doesn't fit. I mean, it does. My finger is the same size. But—" She winces as if the truth is painful. "I wore it here to take a part of the past with me, but I realize that's not how life works."

I remove the paper wrapper from my straw and tie it around her finger. "So no one gets the wrong idea."

She raises her eyebrows.

"You have to watch out for Romeos."

Colette half smiles. "You mean guys like you?"

I set my utensils down. "Colette, when will you realize that I'm not—?" But then I remember we're taking this slow. Letting it unfold and flow. Instead, I say, "What do you mean guys like me?"

"You collect a new admirer at each stop."

"I don't collect anyone. I'm not interested."

"But they're interested in you." She gestures vaguely toward the cashier.

"There's something that you need to know about me," I say seriously.

She straightens as if preparing for bad news.

It may be, depending on her response.

"My real name isn't Antonio. It isn't Romeo either."

Those perfect lips of hers turn down.

"My real name is Pinistro," I say it the Italian way.

"Oh," she says as if it's no big deal.

"Say it."

"What?" she asks.

"Just say it out loud."

She repeats my name with her American English accent. "Oh," she repeats then presses her lips together to quell laughter.

I smile to let her know it's okay. "It's hard not to chuckle, but that wasn't always the case, at least for me. When kids in grade school caught wind of the names of certain body parts in English, they laughed. In high school, they teased. You can imagine how well that went over when I did a semester abroad in the United States. So I started using my middle name."

"Antonio."

I don't tell her all the other things I changed about myself too.

"That's harsh," she says.

"It's hard to believe that no one mentioned to my mother and father to pick a different name. My parents must've hated me before I was born." My father certainly does.

"But when you say it with your accent, it doesn't sound vulgar or silly," Colette says.

"That's sweet of you to say, but—" I hold my hands out, palms up.

She tilts her head from side to side as if she understands my point.

"I'm going to tell you something else about myself."

She leans in as if preparing for more hilarity.

"Colette, no matter who's looking at me. I only have eyes for you. You are *my* woman on the boat. You are the subject of my poems. Of my love letter."

Her throat moves with a swallow and her lips drop open.

"And in case you were wondering, no, my last name isn't Fartio."

She cracks a smile and we both laugh.

Nope. My last name is worse, but I took my shot, laid the truth bare. Now she knows.

But the fact that she doesn't reply, makes me worry that I grabbed the keys to the Lamborghini instead of the Fiat.

After another two hours on the train, intermittently napping and watching the passing farmland, we reach Copenhagen.

"Let's wander. Let's get lost. Let's discover Copenhagen," I say.

A woman with long blond hair and tattoos covering both arms turns around. "You've never been?"

There's a moment of eye contact. Ordinarily, the stranger and I might trade flirtatious smiles, but I say, "I'm showing my girlfriend the city for the first time."

Colette laces her hand in mine. This time, I don't feel like I made a mistake and used the wrong word. Maybe we're driving an average car—like a Chevrolet. Those are popular in the States.

"In that case, you'll want to know all the best restaurants and food stalls." She goes on to list them before we exit opposite a glowing sign advertising Tivoli Gardens. Gleeful screams carry through the walls.

"It's an amusement park. Should we get tickets? Or we could go to the museums, Christianborg Palace, Nyhavn, the harbor area. I think we could visit the house where Hans Christian Andersen lived. Or the Little Mermaid statue," I say, rattling off some of the famed tourist spots.

"I thought you wanted to wander, discover, get lost," Colette says, repeating my comment before we left the train.

"Yes, but this is a bucket list stop. Isn't there something specific you wanted to see?"

"Marcus's great-grandparents were from Denmark. He wanted to see his roots, I guess. I'm happy to wander, discover, and get lost. I imagine that was his plan, anyway."

"Okay, to do that, you have to cover your eyes."

She nibbles her lip. "I already fell in a trashcan once since meeting you. I don't want to take any risks."

"Just trust me."

Colette's palms press over her eyes as I spin her in a circle. When I stop, we're facing the harbor so we wander, discover, explore. And at least for me, I get lost in her smile, her curiosity. Her beauty.

Despite the cool start to the day, as lunchtime approaches, the temperature heats up. We pass cafes studded with condensation beading on people's beverages.

"Hungry?" I ask when the smell of yeasty dough tempts us into a restaurant called *Mother* but in Danish. "This seems like a heart-stomach kind of place."

Servers pass, carrying trays of pizzas fresh out of the brick oven and covered with olives and fresh mozzarella.

"I have come home," I say.

The host, dressed in tight jeans and with gelled hair, explains the communal seating and gestures for us to take a seat at one end of an already occupied picnic table outside. Two guys, nursing dark lager, sit at the other end.

"I want one of everything," Antonio says, ogling the menu.

"When was the last time you were in Italy?"

"Too long."

"Why did you leave?"

But before I can come up with an answer, the server, blond and with tattoos, asks what we'd like to order.

"One of everything," I say.

She smiles coquettishly.

I turn to Colette. "How about we order the *burning love* pizza? It has potatoes, fried onions, mozzarella, and smoked meat."

"When in Copenhagen..." Then she says, "I don't mind wandering. But we should do one big thing while we're here."

"You're looking for something fun to do?" says the guy from the other end of the table. He has a short ginger beard and a Danish accent.

"Yeah. We only just arrived today," I answer.

"Where are you coming from?" the other guy asks. He's athletic with bronze skin, tattoos, and straight teeth.

The way he looks at Colette sets my teeth on edge.

She answers, "Amsterdam, before that London."

"How long are you staying?" the first guy asks.

"Until tonight. Next stop, Stockholm."

"Nice. I'm Maddox," the tattooed guy says.

"And I'm Chris."

We introduce ourselves and talk about travel until our food and a girl, with a French braid and a pair of denim cutoffs, sits next to Chris. She's Simone, his girlfriend and they loop her into our plans.

"You must come with us. We're going to the harbor baths," she says.

After we finish our pizza, we follow the others toward the Islands Brygge. The breeze and passing bicycles shuffle and reshuffle our group, with all of us taking turns chatting.

From up ahead, I hear Maddox say to Colette, "So, you and Antonio—?" Never mind my teeth being on edge, my muscles tense. My gaze hardens because he's really asking if anyone will stand in his way of pursuing her.

I push my shoulders back, but my heart stops as I wait for Colette's answer.

CHAPTER 17
NOT FOR THE FAINT OF HEIGHT
COLETTE

"Yes, me and Antonio, my boyfriend," I answer Maddox's question and glance over my shoulder at my Italian. I extend my hand for him to take.

I feel wild, reckless saying that. Like I'm standing up in the back of a convertible as it cruises down an empty road with the music cranked.

But Antonio's palm fits snuggly in mine and the smile I get, different than the one he gave Izzy, Samantha, the girl on the ferry, or anyone else, is one all my own.

It only took us three countries to admit this, but I'm his girlfriend and he is my boyfriend. I'd like to shout it to any girl whose gaze lingers a little too long and finish it off with, *End of story*! *Back off*! Then maybe roar like a lioness.

When we reach the harbor, the sun lowers in the sky, silhouetting an angular, wooden construction that resembles the front of a ship jutting out of the water.

"You just have to jump in, it's the most refreshing thing you'll ever experience," Maddox tells us. He pulls off his T-shirt.

Simone guides me to a changing room.

"You're going to love this," she says.

"Heights and love don't fit together in my language." But there's another name that does...

"Just don't look down," she says from the neighboring stall as she changes. We stash our belongings in a locker.

Back outside, Antonio and the others wait for us, all talking casually in their swim trunks. The two Danish guys resemble tube socks. *No offense fellas, but you need some sunshine.* My southern sensibilities understand the importance of a healthy glow. Plus, it's summer for goodness sakes. Soak in that Vitamin D while you can!

When my new boyfriend turns I stare. I gape. I might start catching flies if I don't shut my mouth.

Forget the man's hands. His abs are a work of art. The sculpture in those famous London museums I visited last week have nothing on Antonio's chisel.

He smirks. But then I realize he's taking a long sip of me...in a bikini. Not my first choice of swim attire, considering my legs are in dire need of a razor and it's my least flattering bathing suit —thanks for the help, Hazel. But she packed me a single bag, claiming more than that would weigh me down and it wasn't like I was going to Antarctica—even there, I might find some modern amenities.

Speaking of amenities...

Antonio wears that smolder of his and I want to tell him there's nothing else he needs to do to win me over. Signed, sealed, and delivered, baby.

But then Simone has Chris's hand then takes mine and I take Antonio's and we're an accordion of people rushing up to the top of the platform before I can talk myself out of it.

The line of people waiting to jump into the water below stops me. What if I fall and crack my head? No one knows where I am. My phone is glitching—I tried to get it fixed, but the poor robot lady may have taken on a bit too much water. I could disappear forever. My stomach flips at the thought. Then, when I reach the edge, looking all the way down, it does a backflip. I bite my lip and stagger backward. "I'm not too sure..."

Simone nods, assuring. "Don't worry. I've done this before."

Chris says, "Come on, it'll be fun."

Antonio grips my hand. "You got this."

And maybe I do. Perhaps this detour in the trip was unexpected, but so far I've managed and I'm having a good time. I'm not the same person I was when I left, barely able to get out of bed. Lamenting loss. Marcus, yes, but also maybe saying goodbye to the girl I was—letting her go. Now, I'm permitting myself to dream. To fly. Not to mention I've met the guy of my dreams. If the guy of my dreams was the cover model for a glossy European fashion magazine.

But he is. Antonio is real.

And his hand is warm in mine.

I flash a smile and then leap. We go together, whooping all the way down.

When I reach the surface, I draw a deep breath, smoothing my hair from my face. It's refreshing and washes the city grit and sleepy train rides from my skin.

Antonio's buoyant smile meets mine. He wraps me in a wet hug as we tread water. I could float here forever.

"Want to jump again?" he asks.

Our gazes lock. No, I can think of something else I'd like to do again but not here. Not with everyone around. Our first second kiss will be just for the two of us without anyone shining a flashlight and telling us to move along.

Without a second thought, we rush up the structure. The others wait up there too. We laugh like the children in the smaller pools as we jump together in different configurations, take solo leaps, seeing who can make the biggest splash, and Antonio even does flips—of course, he can do flips.

When the setting sun streaks the sparse clouds lavender and iris over the harbor, I shiver and Antonio pulls me close in a one-armed hug.

"You don't want to catch a cold. Come back with us and warm up," Simone offers, looping her arm in mine.

After showers and changing clothes, the five of us settle around an outdoor fire on the patio at Chris and Simone's apartment. We order takeaway and learn about their custom T-shirt business. Our time to leave and head back to the train station comes too soon.

"If you're ever in Manhattan, give me a call." I try my phone but get a gray screen. Then again, I don't know when I'll be going back to New York...or who I'll be when I do. Having reached these northern latitudes, I'm slowly acclimating to a different version of myself.

If I'm a caterpillar and this trip is my cocoon, I'm sure to turn to goo soon and emerge changed. I'm bubbly with it, effervescent with possibility.

At least, that's the feeling I get when Antonio gazes at my lips now and every time since I said one simple word. *Boyfriend.*

The train sighs when we board as though disappointed we're leaving Copenhagen so soon.

I get a whiff of soap and cologne when Antonio lowers into the seat beside me.

"Did you have a good day?" he asks.

"It was fun."

"Like a love letter?"

"Mine would start like this, *Dear Antonio...*"

He kisses my cheek and then nuzzles my neck as the city lights fade into stars as we trundle north. The carriage goes dark for a blink when we enter a tunnel linking Denmark and Sweden.

Antonio's amused smile is soft in the safety light flickering along the aisle.

I tip my head against the seat. "Thank you."

His fingers curl around mine.

I still have the straw wrapper from the ferry ride tucked in my bag. The key chain from Whitehall. And him.

I have Antonio.

He closes his eyes.

But I can't rest. I'm still energized from the cold water in the harbor, exhilarated from jumping, and anticipating the next stop and where it may lead me. Us.

Eventually, I must doze off because the next thing I know I wake to, "*Buongiorno.*"

For a moment, I think we're in Italy but then remember our destination. Stockholm.

I stretch, my neck aching. My back stiff. My head throbbing. "I think I need to sleep in a real bed soon. I like all this spontaneity, but two nights on a train and I'm knickered." My cheeks tint pink. "I meant knackered. You know, like the British say. Not like underwear." I'm still embarrassed he saw mine back in London. If I could fit under one of the train seats like when I hid under the table in Copenhagen I would.

Antonio's smirk dawns. "Should we overnight in Stockholm?"

"Let's see where the day takes us."

"That's the spirit."

When we exit the central station, clouds lie low over the city matching the stately buildings casting everything drab. It makes me want to nap. Or that could be the general lack of sleep catching up with me.

"Shall we wander?" Antonio asks.

The only break in the concrete is a waterway we cross.

"This isn't what I expected," I say.

"From the most expensive city in the world?"

"Is that true?" I balk.

"So I've heard."

"I don't understand what the big deal is."

"Let's give it a chance," Antonio says, linking his arm in mine. "There are two things we should do while we're here. The Photografiska—it's a photography museum—and the Public

Library. He stops. Wait. Three." Antonio sniffs the air. "This way," he says, taking me by the hand.

"Where are we going?" I call after him.

"We're missing something."

"Sleep?"

"Coffee." Antonio pulls me down a narrow lane, takes a sharp right opening up onto a large square surrounded by colorful buildings dating from at least the 1800s and older. Antonio spins around and then says, "Aha!"

At the base of an orange building is a door and window festooned in ivy with a chalkboard sign highlighting the day's specials. An older woman and her dog occupy one of the many wooden chairs crammed in front of the cafe. At another, a couple talks intimately, the guy twisting a piece of the girl's hair absently. Students, tourists, and the young and old fill the rest of the seating. From inside wafts the unmistakable scent of fresh roasted coffee beans and cinnamon. I laugh. "You have your priorities."

"Coffee and," he points at the sign, "*Kanelbulle*." He rests his hand on my shoulder and in all seriousness says, "You can tell everything you need to know about a new place by the food and drink." Then he adds, "And you can tell everything you need to know about a person in much the same way."

I take the lone vacant table and people watch until Antonio returns with a grin, two coffees, and a plate with pastries. He passes me the one with the heart drawn in the foam and sets a cinnamon bun between us.

"We have to feed your heart-stomach. A very important task after a long train ride."

"Are you suggesting the way to my heart is through my stomach, Antonio?" I ask with a smirk.

"I'm saying exactly that." His smile is the amused one and tinged with something else. "*Mangia*." He moves the plate in my direction.

"When in Stockholm," I say. This riff off the *When in Rome* saying is becoming my catchphrase.

It's love at first bite. I close my eyes. Now my mind is blown and my perception of Stockholm changes instantly. The soft, buttery dough layered with cinnamon curling together with the exact right amount of sweetness does make this the richest city if the currency is *kanelbulle*.

"Was I right?" Antonio asks, hiding his real smile behind a sip of cappuccino.

"I'll never doubt you again."

A girl with blond hair and a square jaw, seated at a nearly adjoining table, turns and says, "Don't tell anyone I told you, but the *kanelbulle* at Fabrique Stenungsbageri are the best. Actually, tell everyone. I work there, but I hate it when it gets busy and then everyone complains when we run out. It's best to go first thing in the morning. They are perfect, gooey and buttery. I could eat one every day, but then well, I wouldn't be able to fit into my pants." She laughs. "But then again who needs pants?" She's wearing a long skirt.

"Where is this bakery?" Antonio asks, turning up the gigawatts on his smile.

She says a string of directions I don't follow about it being near Mariatorget Park. "Have you been to Soder? It's the best part of the city if you ask me. The shops and restaurants at least. I mean, come here if you're a tourist, but if you want to see Stockholm like the locals, you should come to SoFo. I'm just here because I'm meeting my aunt." She rolls her eyes.

"We just arrived this morning," Antonio says.

"Where are you coming from? Wait. Let me guess. Italy."

We tell her about our travels and then she explains something called *Mika*, a Swedish pastime that's similar to a siesta. "Come to the bakery and have coffee and *kanelbulle* tomorrow morning. You'll love it."

We thank her and then wind through the quaint, romantic

streets of *Gamla Stan*, the oldest part of the city. Musicians play on the street corners, delightful smells greet us from florists, and nearly everyone I see holds hands in pairs. It's a good day to be in love.

Not a good day to be exhausted though. All this travel catches up with me. I'm dizzy with the need to sleep—running on nothing more than caffeine, adrenaline, and Antonio's good looks.

"We're almost exactly halfway between the library and the museum, which way?" Antonio asks as we move through a crowd in a square with a fountain.

"To a bed," I say, the coffee having done little to wake me up. Then I hear my name through the buzz of passersby. Or at least I think I do.

"Colette, Colette."

I spin, trying to locate the source. I must be experiencing whatever happens when a person is beyond tired, thinking I heard my name. Then I hear it again. It gets louder as the thundering of footfalls nears.

We stop. Antonio and I both looking around, sandwiched between the incoming and outgoing pedestrians.

"Colette." A pair of green eyes meet mine. John Trotman stands in front of me, his chest heaving as he catches his breath. "I thought that was you."

CHAPTER 18
GOAT-FISH-MAN
ANTONIO

A stubby guy who resembles a goat with a skinny ponytail and scraggly beard wraps Colette in a sweaty hug. She stands there stiffly for a long moment and then awkwardly pats him before staggering back. Heat spreads across her cheeks as if caught out past curfew.

They both start talking at the same time and then pause together. They start again and then stop before dissolving in laughter. Hers seems nervous, but I can't be sure. It's sickeningly adorable. It's clear they were a thing at some point in the past—with the way he looks at her with barely veiled, arrogant possession. Or maybe that's just his general personality.

Am I jealous? We'll see where this little encounter goes.

"What a surprise. What are you doing here?" They say a variation of those words at the same time.

"You look so different," Colette says.

"You do too. Summer looks good on you." He chuckles.

How nice of him to notice.

"I haven't seen you since—" the guy starts.

She clears her throat. "Right. Since that baseball game."

"You said you weren't feeling good and—"

"Yeah, those hot dogs. Let me tell ya. Then I got busy with

work and time slipped away." Colette waves her hands like it was unbelievable.

I'm on edge.

"But now you're here. Traveling?" The guy sizes me up as if deciding whether or not he he can take down a lion.

He's the one who has an unkempt wildness about him and looks like he's just emerged from the woods after not having access to a shower for weeks.

Colette seems to snap back into focus and then clings to my arm, hugging it. "This is Antonio. He's also a photographer and my boyfriend." She emphasizes that last part.

I cool off and extend my hand to shake.

"John Trotman," he says.

More like Trout-man. His hand in mine is like a limp fish. I half expected him to have a hoof. A goat-fish?

"I'm a photographer. Nature and adventure travel now, but I used to do print. Supermodels mostly." He waggles his eyebrows. "You're a photographer? I've never heard of you."

"Antonio Moretti," I say. Likely, he's heard of my father if he's been in the art world at all. "Where'd you meet?" I ask. Colette never mentioned anything about modeling. She's gorgeous, but not particularly tall.

John's smile is lumberjack wanna-be arrogance. "It was a blind date. Love at first sight."

Colette starts to shake her head. "A blind date. Yes. My friend Hazel set it up. She fancies herself an amateur matchmaker. The other part—" Her expression wrinkles and creases with discomfort.

He pulls out his phone. "Hazel is going to go wild."

"Hazel," he says into his phone. "You're not going to believe who I'm with."

At the sound of a female British voice guessing the names of her favorite celebrities, Colette grabs the phone from him.

"It's me, Colette. Two words. Pizza B.O. My phone fell in a toilet in Copenhagen and I'm with the Italian. I've gotta go."

At that, she practically pulls my arm out of its socket and we take off across a plaza. It's like we're making a getaway from a jewel heist. I can't say that I'm entirely unfamiliar with that particular activity. Only, this company is much preferred to my father's thugs.

Colette glances over her shoulder as the crowd closes around Trotman who's still on the phone.

When we slow, she chuckles and says, "Little does he know that Hazel is happily married."

"Not that it's any of my business, but what were you saying about pizza B.O.?" I may have purposefully gotten some American expressions wrong, but this one is new to me. "I'm Italian. I like pizza. I feel like this is something I should be aware of."

At that, she bursts into laughter and then slides her hand down her face. "This is so embarrassing. I've turned the other way down streets to avoid that guy. I once made up a story about being on probation and having to stay home to get out of a date. Said that most restaurants in the city had banned me." She winces. "I know, I know. Horrible of me, right? He was just so persistent."

"I can see that."

"He was a total dud, but I played it up because I didn't want any of my friends to realize I was still grieving. It seemed too long."

"Where'd you get that idea?"

She looks down as she shrugs.

I gently grip her shoulder. "I'm no expert, but here's what I think about love and grief. You hold onto the love and keep it in your heart. Some days you will be overcome with it. Sometimes you will sleep the day away, not eat, and only ask yourself why it hurts so much. The grief lingers, coloring moments. Sometimes coloring outside the lines and bleeding into others. Other days you won't be able to sleep and all you can do is cry. Time passes. It shifts. You might call to the other room to ask the person a question only to be devastated by the realization they won't answer. Life will resume with a strange vacancy and then you might go hours or days, weeks even, only to realize you hadn't thought of them once. This will torch guilt, igniting a new kind of ache and a fear that you will forget their face, their voice, the way they made you feel."

Tears brim in Colette's eyes.

I hug her close, kissing the top of her head.

"Then more time will pass and you'll find new things and people and places to love. Let them into your heart. The old loves will still be there. You can hold their place. You won't ever forget."

She's quiet for a long beat. She sniffs and says, "There never really has been anyone since Marcus. I made up dates and stories as excuses. One lie led to another. Snowballed. I have to make it right with my friends."

"Start with me. I want to hear how awful this Trotman guy was and while you're at it, you can brief me on everything you plan to tell your friends about how great I am," I tease, trying to make her feel better. "First, I'll tell you about my dud. I spent a semester abroad in the U.S. It was a glimpse into real life. Not my father's world. I met a sweet girl. Fell in love. So I thought. We made plans to be together after graduation. She was going to visit. Never happened. Then I saw on her social media...It turned out she met someone during spring break. Didn't hear from her ever again. I was crushed."

"If you still have her contact info, I'll track her down and—" Colette tips her head from side to side. "Cover her car with salami."

We both crack up with laughter.

She tells me how she and Trotman had a few dates and she went along with it because Hazel made the match. "Sometimes her love-heart arrow is a hit...and sometimes it's a disastrous miss. That was one of those times."

"What was so bad about him?" Other than everything.

"The pizza B.O. for one."

I lift an eyebrow in question.

"B.O. stands for body odor. Pizza B.O. is the particular stench of an American-style pizza with raw onions. Delicious if you're ordering late-night takeaway with your friends. Disgusting if the guy you're with reeks of it and insists on keeping his arm wrapped around you in a chokehold."

I lower my arm.

She hefts it back into place. "No, silly. Not you."

"So I don't have pizza B.O.?"

She takes a deep breath and sighs contentedly. "No, you smell like expensive cologne and comfort." She nestles closer.

I warm through. "You smell like magnolias and moonlight. Like home."

"Where's that?"

I take a moment to think. "My food-heart misses Italy. My skin misses the golden sun. This far north, the light has more of a silver quality."

"What about your heart-heart?" Colette asks.

My thoughts fall in and out of focus as I lean toward Colette, closing the distance between us. I balance between the itchy discomfort of the unfamiliar and unknown and feel myself falling into her voice, deep brown eyes, and her lips.

We're a whisper apart and I say, "My heart-heart is wherever you are." My pulse races.

She tucks her head, gazing at the ground between us.

We don't kiss.

Is the girlfriend-boyfriend label not enough?

I'm afraid to ask.

Is the offer to give her my heart not enough?

I tell myself that a kiss isn't everything.

But my stomach knots and my brain warns me that once again, I'm experiencing unrequited love.

The next morning we get *kanelbulle* and coffee at the bakery the girl mentioned yesterday. It's even better than she described. We spend the morning at the *Asplund,* a booklover and photographer's fantasy. I pull out my camera and get a few candid shots of Colette when she's not paying attention. The light loves her and I memorize the contours of her cheeks, dotted with freckles. The slope of her nose. And the perfect pillows of her lips.

Then we go to the Fotografiska—a photography museum. Colette asks me about my love of taking pictures.

"I like shots of people and places, mostly. Moments. If you pay attention, no matter where you go, you can spot love. Like right there." I point to a leaf curled like a heart.

"You're such a romantic."

"Is that a bad thing? Like pizza B.O.?"

She snort-laughs through her nose then practically convulses to keep it down so we don't get kicked out. The docent already asked us to be quiet once.

"No, Antonio. Seeing life through a pair of rosy, heart-shaped sunglasses isn't a bad thing at all." She reaches into her bag and pulls out a pink pair, putting them on. She lifts them up and down in my direction and winks like in the movies.

This time I want to laugh. No, I want to pick her up and spin her around in a bear hug. But we proceed to the next collection of photos like adults and not two teenagers in love.

She whispers. "Hazel packed them. I blame everything on Hazel. And before you ask, no, that's not a bad thing. Not at all."

It was this friend of hers who hooked her up with Trotman and who practically forced her to take the trip. The latter was a very good decision.

As we exit, I say, "Anticipation is my favorite. My second favorite is forgetting about the passage of time, space, thought. That's how you know you love something—you lose track of minutes, hours, sometimes even days."

"Is that how you feel when you're taking pictures?"

"Sometimes. But mostly when I'm with you. It doesn't feel like we've only known each other for weeks."

"More like years or like my whole life was leading to right now," she whispers.

Her dark eyes meet mine. Again, I feel the spark, electricity lighting between us.

"Who's the romantic now?" I ask.

She smirks.

We pause in a park. Colette takes one of my curls between her fingers. "It forms a heart shape."

I pull out my camera and pass it to her. "Shoot away."

She snaps a shot then another and another until I'm chasing her. She pauses and stops before I catch up, caging her in my arms. She giggles.

This is another moment when we could kiss, but we don't. My spirits dip.

Her eyes sparkle then she calls, "Look! A heart." She picks up a rock and puts it in my hand.

"See? Love is everywhere."

We wander back toward the high street and split a smorgasbord. The pile of lingonberries bleed into a pink heart. She points it out. I spill my water on the lacquered table, and it leaves a heart-shaped bubble.

"There's another one." I point.

But what about Colette's heart? Is there love there for me?

Afterward, we wander some more. Every few blocks she spots hearts. Street art with hearts. A dog with a heart-shaped collar. A little girl flying a heart-shaped kite.

"Are you noticing this?" she asks. "Love is everywhere."

"Yes. Where will your heart take you next?" I ask, catching her hand in mine.

"I have one more stop on the bucket list. Paris."

"Any movies you've been wanting to see?"

"Uh, I don't know."

"The flight to Paris is about the length of a movie." Will she want me to go there with her though?

"Is what we're doing normal?" Colette abruptly asks.

"Holding hands?"

She shakes her head slightly. "Traveling like this. Not-adulting. I haven't done laundry, paid bills, or done adult stuff in a while. This feels like a fantasy."

I chuckle. "That stuff is overrated, anyway. Let this be a little oasis. A holiday. Summer vacation to you. You'll get back to adulting sooner than you'd like."

"That's what I'm afraid of," she mutters.

After the short flight, we wake up to a pearly sunrise in Paris. A woman wearing a starched white uniform and red lipstick greets us at a nearby hotel.

I'm afraid if Colette doesn't sleep in a real bed soon I might find her curled up under a table at a restaurant instead of hiding under one.

With a gleaming smile, the receptionist says, "Honeymoon? We have special packages for newly married couples."

We peruse a menu of the services available.

"I could use a massage," Colette says.

I belatedly answer the woman, eager to offer us congratulations. "Uh, no. Not a honeymoon."

"Oh. Well, whatever your reason for staying with us, we want to make your time as enjoyable as possible. Please do take advantage of our many amenities and services."

"I was just hoping to sleep in a real bed," Colette mumbles.

We get room keys and pass through double glass doors to an old-fashioned elevator.

"Everything about this place has Parisian charm, but I have to admit it's lost on me at the moment." Colette's eyes droop toward closed.

"Sweet dreams," I say, kissing her on the forehead.

Just before she disappears into her room, she says, "Do you believe in destiny?"

"Like a destination?"

Her eyebrows twitch with curiosity like she hadn't quite thought of it that way before. "I meant like fate, but maybe that's really what destiny is, a destination where you belong."

"Or with who you belong," I add. "To me, that's living the love letter."

We could kiss and remember this always, a photograph on our hearts. I go down the hall to my room, but the door won't open.

CHAPTER 19
LOCKED OUT
COLETTE

I'm dragging on my feet as I collapse onto the bed. My eyes slam shut.

Sleep. Sweet sleep.

Then someone knocks on the door. It's a light rap. Must be a dream.

Need. Sleep please.

It sounds again.

My brain is pure fuzz as I open the door to find Antonio standing there with his hand in his pocket and his bag slung over his shoulder.

"Miss me already?"

His smolder is like a hit of pure caffeine. *Sleep? Is that something I should know about?*

"I'm locked out of my room." His voice is low, scratchy.

I step aside, letting him in.

We could've shared a room, to begin with, to save money.

He could've gone to the front desk and asked to be let in.

I could've ignored his knocking and passed out in ten seconds.

But I'm exhausted or whatever comes after that. Half dead on my feet?

Instead, I plop onto the bed, still fully clothed, curl up, and close my eyes.

The door closes softly. The sound of shoes being toed off, a belt coming loose, and footfalls drift in and out of my awareness.

The bed shifts with Antonio's weight as he settles in behind me. Like a perfect gentleman, he drapes one arm across my shoulder and hugs me close.

And at last, I rest.

I wake to the soft hum of an inhale and exhale. Cars motoring by. Pigeons cooing at the window. I could be anywhere in the world, but right now I feel most at home in Antonio's arms.

His hand snugs around me and I study the lines of his wrists and the heavy, expensive watch he wears. Then I trace his knobby knuckles. A scar, a few shades paler than the rest of his tan skin, runs from the space between his thumb and first finger then toward the middle. In the various cities I've visited, I've seen signs for palm reading. I think this side of Antonio's hand could tell more stories than the lines and creases on the other. They're strong hands. Capable. I lace my fingers through and wonder what his fourth finger would look like with a ring looped around it.

A warm, buttery feeling comes over me. Everything is so right in this moment. If I could have him take a photo of it, capture it forever, I would.

But life is fleeting.

Accidents happen.

Decisions must be made.

As I lay there, I wonder what this trip would've been like had it been Marcus and me. We'd have been tourists. On the outside looking in.

With Antonio, I'm a traveler, an explorer. We experience new places, tastes, and sights in a way I couldn't with anyone else.

I miss Marcus terribly. I'll always love him and what we had, but I'm starting to wonder if it's time to move on. To roll over and kiss Antonio madly on the lips. I've been holding back, wanting to honor my previous husband and our relationship. But when do I give myself over to this love I feel for Antonio and start a new relationship?

How will I know? Paris was supposed to be the last stop on the bucket list. Then what? Do I go back to Manhattan? Travel to Italy as I've always wanted to do?

My stomach grumbles.

Antonio rouses and in a sleepy voice says, "You need a crepe. With chocolate. Maybe more than one."

I laugh. "Good morning to you too. Or should I say *bonjour*?"

He jiggles his wrist, adjusting his watch so he can read it. "More like evening."

"This European sleep schedule won't work for me when I go back to the office." But the words are like putting on someone else's shoes. They don't fit. I risk getting blisters. However, I can't very well become a vagabond, traipsing all over the world. Granted, Hazel and Maxwell's travel points helped and sleeping on trains has saved on hotels, but I still have expenses and my apartment in Manhattan.

"That seems like another world. Another life," I say vaguely.

"Have you thought about going back?" Antonio asks.

I stuff my head under the pillow and give a muffled, "I'd rather not."

A long beat passes when he doesn't say anything. I don't want him to—afraid he might ask me to stay. So I pick up the pillow and whack him with it.

He blinks once, twice and then picks up the other pillow, bashing it into my thigh. We go back and forth, pillow-fight style.

He takes my hands in his, pulling me to my feet to stand on the bed. Like we're five years old he starts bouncing. As my feet leave the earth for one second and then two, I have that feeling of lightness again, like when we jumped from the platform and into the water back in Copenhagen.

I can't help it, I start laughing and Antonio too and then tears stream from my eyes, and for those moments I'm free.

I stand up on my knees and clobber him so he falls back. I give him another few thwacks with the pillow for good measure.

With each one, in my head, I say, *Antonio, don't like me too much. Don't make this more difficult.* Then, *I want to stay, but I'm scared.*

But it all feels too big for me to contend with, so I double down and mush the pillow against his upper half.

"Are you trying to smother me?" he asks.

I laugh because that would make things easier in the short term—I wouldn't have to face these huge and confusing feelings.

This mountain of a man grips my outer arms, pinning them to my sides and then flips me over. He hovers above, his messy curls forming a curtain. Our eyes meet. Hold.

Even though we're just waking up, Antonio still smells like expensive cologne and comfort. Even when his hair is out of place, it's perfect.

His gaze drops to my lips.

I want him.

He wants me.

But I don't think I'm ready to go there because once I do, there's no going back. I'll be stuck to this man like southern humidity sticks to skin in August. Not the prettiest analogy, but at least I didn't say *moist* or *damp*. Ew. Those are two gross words. And enough to distract me from going further.

At least, for now.

Is it possible to kiss someone in your mind so many times that you can feel the warmth, the longing, the deliciousness of it? There was the kiss under the bridge so I have the gist of an Antonio Moretti smooch. But my memory combined with my imagination is probably almost as good as the real thing, right?

This is Marcus's trip. The thought is like a blowing out a candle.

I roll over. "You were saying about crepes?" I ask, but my

heart isn't in it. It's straggling twenty seconds behind when the intensity in Antonio's eyes told me only one thing would satisfy his heart...and his food-heart.

Me.

He sits up and drags his hand through his hair. Never mind smothering him, I might be killing him. But the time isn't right. Not yet.

"I'm going to shower and then we'll grab some food, okay?" I ask.

He quietly gathers his things and leaves, presumably to sort out his key issue. Either that or the woman at the front desk misheard about our honeymoon and stuck us in the same room —or saw the connection between us. The one I can't deny. At least, not for much longer.

After a long shower, I pull on a sundress with blue stripes. Very Parisian.

The rumble of Antonio's voice in the hall draws me into the hallway as he talks to a porter, thanking him for helping him with the key earlier. His damp curls hang around his face. Freshly showered, his yummy scent game is strong.

"Ready for the last stop on your bucket list?" he asks.

I'm not and I am. Both.

I don't want this trip with Antonio to be over. But I'm not sure where to go next. What to do?

Refreshed and on the street, we get on the Metro to go to the city center.

Antonio turns to the man next to us, "Where can we get the best crepes in Paris?"

He shakes his head and mutters a curse in French.

I try again, this time in his language, which I speak fluently.

The man fixes his eyes on the middle distance as if to say he doesn't want to bother with me. My accent isn't that bad, is it?

A young woman, dressed in a pencil skirt and with red lips, wears a knowing smirk. She brushes him off. In French, she gives us directions to a place off Avenue Anatole France.

I don't hear the rest of what she says because she whisks off to her stop. I shrug my shoulders. "She also said something about going to a park?"

When we emerge from the Metro, it's dark, but Paris isn't asleep. I feel newly born as if I'm seeing the world for the first time. My heart and my mind are both wide awake, taking it all in. Paris was my bucket wish list item. Taxis whiz by, pedestrians dart across streets, and I smell bread, the hint of rain, and trash.

The last part wasn't exactly the romantic Paris of my dreams, but there were dreams I didn't know I had and they start with the man who clasps my hand.

Antonio and I meander down the streets until we see a crepe stand. In French, I order one with Nutella and Antonio gets one with eggs and cheese. While we wait, Antonio says, *"Mon amour!"* His voice curls around the words.

Mon amour? My love.

"Vous sentez comme noix de coco et pamplemousse."

"It's the soap," I answer, when he says I smell like coconut and grapefruit.

This is what it's like to really flirt with a hot European guy. Can't say I mind. Not a bit. He could pinch my fanny and I probably wouldn't complain.

"Je vous te goûter." Antonio nips my earlobe after saying that he wants to taste me. I shiver with anticipation. I wrap my arms around him and tilt my head back.

I want to kiss him. So badly, but I'm supposed to be here with Marcus.

On the wall opposite, there's a mural of a girl sitting in a green field, holding one lonely daisy, hanging onto the threads of summer, of possibility. It is then I know with certainty that all the daisies in all the fields in all the world couldn't answer the question *He loves me, he loves me not*. Yes, of course, he loves me.

And I love him.

Could I say it in English? French maybe?

But our crepes are ready. We swap bites, once more, the

moment lost. I've had so many opportunities slip past—to tell Antonio how I feel and for us to kiss.

I'm scared.

The imp on my shoulder tells me we're not meant to be.

The cherub on the other one tells me that I'm just taking it slow.

Then the *boom* of fireworks, somewhere nearby, light up the night.

The imp and the cherub take to the sky, leaving me with my confusing and conflicting thoughts.

What's stopping me? What's holding me back?

The bucket list burns hot in my pocket.

Antonio takes my hand, leading me deeper into the city. We follow a horde of people toward a park where the sky opens in a blaze of light with the Eiffel Tower rooted to the ground, reaching for the glittering heavens.

Antonio spins me around in his arms. We're both laughing until I'm pretty sure I sprain a stomach muscle.

A million twinkling, star-like explosions shower down on us like rain burning away the past and lighting the way for the future.

I recall the first thing Antonio said to me and realize that *ciao* means goodbye and hello. It's time for me to say both.

CHAPTER 20
LOCKED IN
ANTONIO

The next morning Colette and I step into the Parisian sun and walk until we find another crepe stand along the river Seine. Then we walk some more, going everywhere and nowhere together. It's delightful. I bring my camera along, something I usually don't do when I'm traveling with other people, but I take candid photos of Colette every chance I get.

This is also the last stop on her list. What's next for her? For us?

I don't want to miss a moment. I feel a sense of urgency, like time spilling from an hourglass.

We admire the architecture and Notre Dame, watch the street performers, and race alongside the Catamarans and rowboats as they glide through the glassy water. We spend the next days like this, exploring, wandering, and holding hands.

Being with Colette all this time, and especially in this romantic city where we share late-night dinners by candlelight, I want nothing more than to kiss her, but she holds back. Keeps me at a distance.

One afternoon, we reach a bridge I recognize and stop at a nearby kiosk with a marquee that reads *Cadenas d'Amour*. I buy a padlock and marker then lead Colette to the bridge where hundreds, maybe thousands, of padlocks line the fence on either side.

"This is *Pont des Arts.* These are lovelocks," I explain. "The idea is that a couple writes their initials on the padlock, fasten it to the bridge, and then toss the key in the river."

"I've heard of this place—thought they carted away the locks."

"They tried. Love always wins."

"That could be the name of your next photo project."

Hope rises on a tide of love for Colette. But will our love win? It's time to find out.

I sense she's thinking about her late husband. Maybe they planned to visit this place. I uncap the marker, but she takes it from me.

On the back of the lock, she writes the letters *C + M* then circles it with a heart.

My heart craters. My initial is *A*...or *P* for my first name. *M* is for Marcus. This is why she's keeping me at arm's length. She still loves him. Of course, she does. She always will. There isn't room for me.

She fastens the lock on the fence. Pausing for a moment, she closes her eyes and then tosses the key into the water. She says a soft, "*Je t'aime.* I love you."

I turn away at the sound of the key making a *plop.*

Even though this guts me, I don't blame Colette. Marcus was her first love. Probably a great guy. They had plans for their life, their future.

And this time together has been a vacation for her. She'll go back to Manhattan and carry on, forgetting about me. I try not to think about my American ex-girlfriend. How we never saw each other again.

Then a hand slides into mine. Small. Soft. Warm.

"I'm ready." Colette's voice is strong, confident.

She did what she came here to do and is ready to go back to New York, no doubt. Our time together is over.

I give a stiff nod.

She glances back at the bridge as we walk away. "My love for Marcus now has a place to live." She looks up at me. Her eyes are damp but sparkly. "And now you can have the key to my heart if you want it."

My jaw lowers as we continue to walk.

I don't think I heard her right.

"I needed closure. Fitting that we found a lock, a key...and love."

My own heart opens wider and wider as understanding dawns.

We stop on the sidewalk as the world streaks past. Her dark brown eyes meet mine. There isn't a question or curiosity there. Rather, I see demand. All the times we've wanted to kiss funnel into this moment.

She lifts onto her toes.

I grip her low back with one hand and cup her cheek with the other.

She curls into me.

I tip my chin down to meet her lips.

Her glorious lips.

Poetry couldn't describe how this feels.

Not in any romance language.

It is soft and light. Strong and luscious.

Kissing Colette is everything I imagined and more.

It doesn't matter where we are or where we've been. We have this right now.

She presses against me and my pulse matches hers.

I worry about my stubble scratching her and cup her jaw gently between both palms.

She tugs my shirt, pulling me closer.

My hands skim the nape of her neck, down her back, and I obey her command, drawing her in.

I feel her smile against my lips. I feel mine lighting up my face.

It doesn't matter what happens next because everything is finally right in the world, in my life, and in my heart.

I'm kissing the woman of my dreams.

We part naturally, knowing we'll do that again. Kiss on every corner in this city. Maybe backtrack, retracing our steps, and kiss every time we missed all over the continent.

After dinner, we return to the hotel and kiss in the hall before falling through the door and into Colette's room.

We go to the balcony where the sweet summer air breezes. The city sparkles below.

"I'm ready," Colette says, repeating her comment from earlier.

"To kiss again?"

She wraps her arms around my neck and I grip her waist.

"Definitely that, but to leave." Her gaze fixes on me.

Tension ripples through my shoulders. "What do you mean?"

"I think we should go to Italy. I did what I came here to do. All this time, I was being guided by someone else's map, an old version of me. And you still have your mother's journal."

Joy overwhelms me and then a sigh escapes. "I've mostly given up."

She chews her lip as though deciding what to say next. "You may not find your mother, but I'm guessing the rest of your family misses you."

Despite our difficulties, I also miss them. What she said about not being the same person she was is true for me too.

I bypass a kiss and squeeze Colette into a hug. This is but another reason I love this woman. "Will you come with me?"

"I'd be honored," she says.

We took two trains. It's fitting we take two planes. The next morning, we fly into Naples.

Colette's hand remains firmly in mine. My smile is so big at returning home with her by my side that my cheeks ache. I don't care.

Everything from the leaves on the trees to the certain briskness in the air coming off the water to the hum from the streets all matches whatever it is in my veins that attach me to this place; in much the same way we're connected to our relatives and friends even when we're not together. Scientists may not have a name for it, but I feel it. I feel at home.

I feel at home here.

I feel at home with Colette.

"Can I show you my city?"

She beams a toothy grin. "I want you to show me everything."

We leave the airport, pass the university, and street art and sculptures and so much stone. We walk toward the old part of town. The buildings, the streets, and the trees, even the sky, seem slightly smaller than I remember as though I've slid down the rabbit hole with Alice and now inhabit a strange new land, yet it's bigger too and better than I remember.

I haven't been here for years, so I don't know what I was expecting. Fragments of memories come to me, and I try to piece them together with others, from photographs, from the scent of bread and garlic, fresh out of the oven, and from the snatches of conversation I overhear from passersby.

We wind down the cobblestone streets. My steps are sure. My breath steadies and my shoulders relax. We reach a grassy square with a fountain in the middle. The narrow arteries of streets call me to adventure, but I order us coffee and pastries. One of each, like the time Colette got the collection of cookies from the AV Club.

Colette lounges in the grass by the fountain. Her expression is serene. At rest. Like she's finally set down the heavy baggage she'd been carrying. This is the kind of moment I'd like to capture with a picture.

We dig into the coffee and sweets, and she says, "If it's wrong that I want pastries for breakfast and am already thinking about what kind of gelato I want for lunch then I don't want to be right."

I toss my head back and laugh. "Nope. Nothing wrong with that at all. You can make your own rules."

"Tell me three things I need to know how to say in Italian."

"Ok. Hello. *Ciao.*" I leave off the part about how it all means goodbye.

"But I already know that one."

"How are you?" I translate and speak the words slowly. Then we test out responses.

"One more."

"Ti amo." As the syllables peel from my tongue, I know it wholly, with my entire heart, that I love her.

"Ti amo," she repeats. "But I knew that already too."

She slides into my lap, wrapping her arms around me.

"I love you, Colette."

She bites her lip and leans close. Just before she kisses me on the lips, she says, "I love you, Antonio."

We take that and our kisses with us as we meander through the old town and toward where I used to live. Where my family still lives. The triumphant afternoon sun shadows the buildings on one side of the street. The cement turns into cobbles again, and the homes age as though they've been keeping pace with me all this time.

Just before we reach my house, I stop at another café. I have to prepare Colette...and myself. More coffee is required. My family isn't like the way she described her parents and siblings.

"The Morettis may live in the city, but they practically own it...and many sidewalks beyond," I say carefully, not quite sure how to explain the family business. "My father—"

How do you tell someone your father is an art and jewelry

thief and commands half the crime families in Europe? It's not something I'm proud of. But it is something I got away from.

"Your mother," Colette says.

I clear my throat, ready to try again.

She shakes her head. "There's no mistaking her. Antonio, I think that's your mom." Her voice is a whisper as she stares into the room at my back.

I turn slowly, following her gaze to a woman with wrinkles around her dark brown eyes—the same as mine. My father's are blue—rare for a southern Italian but contribute to his mystique.

I feel like I've seen her before.

Time stalls as I get to my feet and step closer. The past ricochets through me. It bounces off scar tissue. It dives into my bones. "Kristy?" I ask.

Her smile is slight, apologetic. "Can I help you?" she asks in perfect Italian.

"My name is Pinistro Antonio Moretti."

Her expression shadows for a minute and then her gaze lifts to mine.

I pull the journal out of my bag and slide it across the counter to her.

Tears fill her eyes as she flips through it and then looks back to me. "I am sorry," she says.

For a moment, I think there's a mistake, and she's not my mother. Then her hand reaches for mine. "Yes, I'm Kristy Nichols and I'm so sorry," she repeats.

I look around at this café I've been in dozens of times—for a cold drink after soccer practice, to plan my father's various shady deals, to meet with girls in high school.

"You've been here all this time?" I ask.

"Watching you grow up."

"But I've been gone for years."

"I knew you'd come back."

"But I thought you'd left."

"It was better for both of us that way." She leans closer. "You must know how your father is."

She gives me a sympathetic expression. Has she forgiven him for taking her baby? I have so many questions. I turn back to Colette and she takes my hand.

I make introductions and then we plan to meet for dinner.

Before we leave the café, my mother says, "Antonio, do you forgive me?"

The word *yes* balances on my tongue, but I don't let it tumble.

The scars my father left haven't faded yet.

Then she says, "I've heard that your father is ill."

My insides freeze. My muscles tighten and I march out of the café, prepared for battle.

I turn to Colette, and say, "I'm sorry."

It's not goodbye, but it's not *ciao* either.

CHAPTER 21
ROMEO, ROMEO, WHERE ART THOU
COLETTE

Antonio suddenly takes off, leaving the café without a backward glance. I stand there starkly, confused. When he doesn't return, I remain there a while longer, waiting.

His mother, Kristy, practically blends into the wallpaper like she doesn't want to be seen. I glean that she works in the kitchen here. From what I've gathered, Romeo Moretti hasn't won any father of the year awards. Dark images from mafia movies come to mind. Kristy probably wanted to remain close to her son without raising any suspicions.

I don't know the whole story. Not even many parts of it. Not sure I want to.

I move outside as the sun sets, washing the stone buildings in golden light. When night crawls in, I ask a couple passing where the nearest and nicest hotel is. I leave a note for Antonio with the young woman behind the register at the café. I make a note to myself to get my phone fixed.

I follow the directions along the cobblestone streets until my shoes echo on the marble floor in the lobby of a hotel that smells like wet paint.

I get a room and try not to wonder what happened to Antonio. I try not to worry about him or about us. My nerves scatter to the corners of the room and hardly let me sleep.

Early the next morning, I return to the café. The sun is so bright it bleaches the paving stones. Dogs bark. Vespas whizz past. I like it here, but I'd like it better with Antonio.

After spending the morning at the same café as yesterday, he doesn't turn up. I inquire at the register several times in case we missed each other.

People sit outside on the patio, talking and laughing in stark contrast to the sinking feeling inside me.

I spend the next two days like this while I wait for my phone to be fixed. Desperate, I ask people if they've seen Antonio. At the mention of his last name, I get a mixture of dubious and dangerous looks.

I wander the city, hoping we'll run into each other like we did so many times in London. I spot plenty of tall, tan men with curly hair but none of them is *my* tall, tan man with curly hair.

But was he really mine?

Was Marcus?

I start to doubt. I'm not destined for lasting love. Rather, fleeting love that goes away too soon. My heart aches. It's been strip-mined. Emptied.

As I make the route back toward the hotel, a couple argues in an alcove. They switch between French and Italian. She accuses him of cheating. That part I understand. I should've known better than to trust a Romeo.

Maybe I left my heart in Paris.

Maybe I should've stayed in Manhattan.

My bags may be light, but I've carried disappointment, confusion, frustration, and hopelessness with me across every kilometer. I can't add another burden to the load. Antonio was the perfect midsummer's night dream. But it's time to wake up.

Lying in bed restless later that night, I make a decision. Antonio gets one more day. If he doesn't turn up, I'm leaving.

The dewy morning air invigorates me and I inhale deeply,

putting the highs and lows of the last days behind me as I return to the café.

Kristy hasn't been here either. Maybe they had a family reunion.

I consult my inner compass as the minutes drag by.

But the new day brings clarity. I fell into a romantic spell. I've been in a time warp or a daze, ceding control over my summer to a handsome Italian.

With a glance back at the café, I start walking. When I reach a crossroads, I have to make a decision. East calls me to fly back to New York or north where my friend Catherine lives in Rome.

I'm torn. Do I pack up my broken heart and return to my misery in Manhattan or do I dust off and continue to travel until I find a place I'd like to land, to put down roots?

For years, I worked as a lawyer, but that's not my dream. That was the plan, and awash in early widowhood, I clung to anything familiar, to the plan I had in order to keep my head above water.

But I'm different now. Maybe a whimsy is exactly what I need instead of a list or a plan or an itinerary.

A stooped man sweeps the sidewalk in front of a bakery. The red and white awning flutters overhead. He pauses and tips his cap as I pass. The smell of baking bread reminds me of comfort.

I stop. "Excuse me. Do you have any cookies?"

The man gives me a funny smile and his lips crinkle into an affirmative.

Inside, I browse the display case. "Please, make that one of each," I say, when the clerk's hand hovers over chocolate amaretti, twisty torcetti, and almond pizelles—I could eat a hundred of those. If they had gelato, I'd have ordered a scoop. It's that kind of day.

I finally had my phone properly repaired the other day, so after, I settle at a bistro table with the cookies and coffee, I send Catherine a photo.

Me: Guess where I am.

Catherine: Someplace delicious. Wish you were here.

She sends a photo of the beach.

Me: As it turns out I'm a few hours south.

Catherine: Wait? Where? What time is it there? Are you eating a cookie for breakfast?

Me: Cookies, plural. Send me your address and I'll be there as soon as I can.

My phone rings and I give her sparse details about the last month. I learn she's on a long weekend in a small seaside town halfway between Naples and Rome.

Maybe fate is offering me a runner-up prize to the sweeping love affair with the handsome Italian—a best friend whose couch I can sleep on and in whose arms I can cry.

I manage to get to the train station and study the map. Catherine is in a place called Sperlonga—sounds like a delicious sandwich from a deli in Manhattan.

In the next hours, I cover every possible option from every angle in terms of what to do next. I close my eyes as the evening commuters bustle by at the various stops. If I were Antonio, where would I go? What would I do?

But that doesn't matter. I'm Colette, and I'm leaving.

Catherine meets me at the station in Sperlonga with a wide-brimmed hat and a sundress. She's the picture of joy and health.

My look is more *dragged out of an alley by a feral cat.*

We exchange small talk until we return to her hotel where we go immediately to the beach and one of those fancy little cabanas in the sand. She orders us drinks with ice and twizzle straws and umbrellas.

"Okay, tell me everything."

I sniffle. "Don't mind me. I got moisturizer in my eyes this morning. They've been blurry all day."

"Oh, sweetie," she says, pulling me in for a hug.

I pick up, stream-of-consciousness style, relaying the last month and the last couple of days.

"Why don't you just call him. Talk to him. Enough of this running into each other and leaving things up to chance."

"Fate? Cupid?" I say hopefully, trying one more time to appease those little love munchkins with their sharp arrows. "Being with Antonio had a romantic rather than a practical, logical quality.

"You're a modern, empowered woman. Take matters into your own hands. Call the guy and communicate like an adult for goodness sake."

"Funny thing, I dropped my phone into a toilet."

At that, Catherine tips her head back in raucous laughter.

It's a much-needed break from the tears I've shed.

"But you got in touch with me so it must work alright," she says, ever rational.

"But that doesn't help me know where to go."

Catherine wears a strange smirk. "Go? No, you're staying. Get ready to call Sperlonga home."

"Sounds like the name of a hoagie. I could definitely go for a grinder, a sub, a footlong. Mmm."

Again, we both laugh. Mine more like a nervous titter. Hers light and airy because she's in love. Well, so am I, but Antonio ditched me just like I predicted he would.

"Where is that romantic marine of yours, anyway?" I ask.

"He's over there, writing." She points a few cabanas down.

"You guys have some life."

She clasps her hands as she drags me through the sand toward the street. "We do and you're going to love it here."

"I guess I could stay a few days," I mutter as a Vespa putters past.

The curling lampposts, the attention to detail on the borders of the buildings, and the smells in the streets distract me as we walk through the quaint town before arriving at *Libri e Caffè al Mare.*

Catherine translates, "Seaside Books and Coffee. It's been here for over thirty years and risks going out of business."

"That's sad. How come?"

"The owner is retiring, and no one has stepped up to take over. Kellan and I spend so much time here we'd hate to see it close."

A smile blooms on my face. "Why don't you buy it? He's an author. You're very entrepreneurial. If the shoe fits..." The expression reminds me of Antonio. Only, he'd probably say something like *If the goo fits* just to make me correct him.

Tears pierce the corners of my eyes. I linger by the door to the café, pretending to read a sign telling the history of the shop. It's in Italian so the letters mostly look like blurry alphabet soup.

Catherine appears at my back. "Huh. The first day they were opened was on your birthday." She points.

"Do you speak Italian now too?"

She nods proudly. "I have a tutor and use an app on my phone." She thrusts a cannoli in my hand.

I wrap my arms around her in a hug. "Thank you for taking care of me."

"Well, you're going to owe me." Her smile is warm.

I've missed my friends so much. As I take a big bite of the crunchy outer layer and creamy filling, my appreciation builds. The food-heart is real.

"You see, we would like to buy this place and run it, but we have the dog adoption app and travel back to the states a lot, so we'd need someone to manage things."

"I'm sure you could hire someone," I say around another mouthful.

We wander over to the display case, filled with pastries and yummy confections. I'm transported to the many cafes Antonio and I visited.

"Do they have gelato here?" I ask.

"Thinking about him?" she says softly.

I nod and tell her all about how we hopped from café to café, talking, eating, flirting...

"Then you're practically an expert." I don't tell her how I waited to kiss him until I'd said goodbye to Marcus.

She turns to me and says, "Sometimes knowing when it's time to let go of a dream is as important as knowing when to go after one."

"I can promise you becoming a lawyer is no longer my dream."

"Then what is?"

"That's the million-dollar question, isn't it?" I sigh.

"No, more like thirty-thousand."

I'm perplexed by her response and am about to correct her but not much makes sense right now anyway, so I wander to the dusty bookshelves. Although this place seems like a local institution, the haphazard shelves and clutter speak to neglect. I imagine the place in its former, cozy glory then picture myself living a life like Catherine's—sunshine, sea breeze, a husband…

I'm at a loss. That's not fate's plan for me, but I don't want to go back to Manhattan. All I can think about there is crawling into my bed and not wanting to leave.

The depression of the last months lifted, but I'm afraid it would close around me like a cage if I were to go back.

I have the sense there's still more for me but where?

"There you are," Catherine says, presenting me with an iced coffee drink. "So what do you think?"

"It's charming. A little dusty. A lot of clutter. But that's fixable."

"My thoughts exactly."

We're near the back of the shop and she holds her fingers out in front of us, framing them like a camera. "You behind the counter, maybe book signings, music, poetry readings, art on the walls."

I sputter, practically choking as the coffee shoots through the straw. "Hold on. Wait up. You said *you*. As in me?"

She claps me on the back. "The proud new manager of *Libri e Caffè al Mare*."

Catherine is joking. She has to be. Too many romance novels, too much sunshine, living this good life. It's gone to her head.

The plain expression she wears that lifts into a bright and hopeful smile don't suggest she's created a fantasy for us to indulge to distract me from my heart woes.

"You're not kidding are you?" I ask.

Her head slides from side to side. "The minute you got here, the idea flew into my mind. Like fate had something to do with this."

I open my mouth then close it, not sure what to say first or whether to accuse the imp, Cupid, or someone else entirely of this treachery.

No way.

This is crazy.

I blurt, "But I don't speak Italian."

"You can learn. And you happen to know someone who does." She nudges me with her shoulder.

"No, I have to forget about him."

Catherine's lips twist like she doesn't believe I will anytime soon. "Well, in the meantime, you start on Monday. Flavio is going to show you the ropes before you take the reins."

"But I'm on summer vacation."

"Time to return to the real world. Well, as real as this little oasis by the sea gets." She winks.

And that is how I spend the next weeks cleaning up the bookstore, the office above, waiting on customers, and learning to make the best espresso south of Rome—at least Flavio says so.

But all the while, my thoughts thread with memories of Antonio, of our time spent in cafes, and I can't help but startle every time the bells to the door jingle signaling the arrival of a new customer.

CHAPTER 22
RECKLESS LOVE
ANTONIO

I'm at a loss. I don't want to be like my father, but I went back home with my fists flying. Meeting my mother was a fleeting joy. Learning she'd been nearby all that time, that I'd been fooled, sent me over the edge. Then that my father was sick threw me for a loop. My brother and I got into it. Bad.

I haven't left the family compound in over a week because of the black eye and bruises. Piero looks worse. I'm not happy to say I haven't missed a step when it comes to slugging it out.

Romeo Moretti raised us with all the finery life has to offer along with a load of lies. But to guard all of that, we had to learn to fight.

Jewel robberies.

Art heists.

Bank vaults.

I've seen it all and I am not proud. I left this world to live an anonymous life. A normal life.

Only, I come back and it turns out I'm not much different.

I wander through the palatial home nestled in the center of Naples, my father's headquarters. I pass through the library and think of Colette. The ballroom. The dining room. The kitchen.

The scent of garlic, basil, and oregano smells like home...almost. But I don't belong here.

I wanted to believe I belonged with her.

Yet, I perch on one of the stools in the kitchen like I always did because where else would I go? I've exhausted myself traveling. I found my mother.

Cruel irony that she was exactly where I started. Crueler that Colette was the one to recognize her.

But I'm the cruelest of all for turning my back on both of them.

Nonna, my grandmother, used to always sit in the corner, helping out. The kitchen contains all my recollections of her. I watch as the cooks prepare the meals for the family and guests. There are always guests involved in my father's shady dealings.

A memory crashes into me. Does Imelda, the woman I learned was my stepmother, know about Kristy? She must. Obviously, I wasn't her kid. How did she go along with my father's infidelities? How could she have loved me? Because the truth is, she did. Never treated me differently than the rest of my siblings.

Another dark thought crosses my mind. Do any of the others have different mothers?

"It'll get better soon," a female voice says in Italian.

I don't need to look up to know it's Imelda. Or as I always called her, *Mama.*

I let out a sigh. "I wish I believed that."

"Your father missed you. Me too. All of us. What made you leave?"

I don't answer.

"What brought you back?"

"A woman."

I can practically hear her eyebrow shoot into the air.

I round on her. "Did you know my mother was here? Is that why you'd always bring me to that café after soccer practice?"

Tears fill Imelda's eyes. "You know how your father is."

"Why hasn't anyone ever stood up to him? Why the cowardice?"

Her eyes flick to mine. "You did. You stood up to him and he's never been the same."

The words sting. "Are you saying that I made him sick?"

Her expression turns stricken. "No. But he changed after the night you two fought and then left. You may not believe this, but he started to clean up the Moretti name."

"I didn't know it was dirty," I spit. I definitely did, but I'm feeling contrary, angsty.

"If you look around, you'll notice some pieces of art are missing." She glances at her hands. "And some jewelry. One day he just tore frames from the walls, raided the safes. He made anonymous donations to museums."

"That doesn't sound like him."

Her eyes soften as she shrugs. "He's old. He's sick. He'd like to see you."

I shake my head like a petulant child. "He's asked for you. I think he's waiting to say goodbye."

This conversation makes my throat feel scratchy. I turn to Imelda, wanting her, or someone, anyone to feel my agony. "I thought if I found my mother, my life would change. I would. But I'm still the same. Colette was right. I'm a Romeo. No different than my father."

"You're nothing like him...and I hope to meet Colette someday."

Not likely. I stalk from the kitchen. Instead, of going to my room, I wander the halls. Imelda was right. Fewer "lost and borrowed" pieces of art fill the walls. I pause in front of a portrait of a pair of hands—mine and Nonna's, taken shortly before she passed away. It's one of my pictures.

I had no idea my father even knew I took photos. Then again, he probably had someone tailing me from the moment I left home.

As I look at Nonna's knobby hand clasping mine, the last

years scroll through my mind, snapshots of people and streets, moments and scenes—connecting with strangers, living and loving. I've wanted my life to be a love letter because if not that, what else is there?

Another truth rushes past the one that chased me here. A truer, brighter, and more beautiful truth.

I love Colette. Every heartache and hardship up until this point led me to her.

In my room, I start writing a letter to Imelda, my mother and father, and Nonna. To America and the first girl to break my heart along with all the ones after that including the hearts that I broke. I include my brother and sisters. All the friends along the way.

Except I don't use paper and pen.

The love letter is me. I take a photo—a selfie as silly as that is. I make a promise to be the best son, brother, friend, and lover I can be.

No matter what.

But first, I have to face my father.

It's nearly dark when I unfold myself from the chair, hunched over the computer and the record of every photograph I've ever taken as I organize them, create a portfolio of sorts.

Colette was right. Love is everywhere. I see it in the way the sunlight reflects off smiles, the twinkle in young eyes and old, the moments of concentration, conflict, and challenge. The laughter and joy. Suffering and tears. So many photos telling stories, love stories.

I pad down the hall into the room at the end. It's blue twilight inside. My father lays in the king-size bed jutting from the wall. I've rarely gone in his room and wonder if Imelda still stays in here.

A nurse closes the door behind her, apparently realizing we'll need a private moment.

"My son. You returned." He's small and tucked under a

heavy blanket even though it's warm out. "I knew you'd come back."

Anger and sadness come at me from opposite sides.

"Where have you been?" he asks.

"I've been falling in love."

He chuckles and then coughs. "Sounds like your old man."

"No, I've been falling in love with life."

"Yes, with life," he repeats.

I don't think of him as having a passion for anything but vice.

"The difference between you and me though is I am like a piece of dynamite. You are like a candle. One explodes. Boom. The other burns slowly, generous with its light." He coughs again, harder this time.

The nurse comes in and tends to him.

It's strange, seeing him vulnerable this way. I sit there a while longer, thinking about vulnerability. The word *ability* hides inside it. Vulnerable has the word *able* in it. Ability and able. What are my abilities? What am I able to do? Love. I can love in my big, passionate way and let myself be loved. For so long, I didn't believe I deserved to be loved in any true, meaningful way. That changed when Colette came along.

I remain there as the moon rises. As a new day comes. I doze in the chair and stay a while longer. My father comes in and out of sleep, tells me stories. Some with happy endings. Others without. I snooze and watch him sleep. After all that travel, all that movement, I'm still. Contemplative. Present.

Then peace washes over me and I know this is the closest I'll ever be to my father. To an apology for his wrongdoings. But that's alright. I forgive him.

At last, I get up and squeeze his hand. "I'm leaving again, Papa."

"I know. Go tell that girl how much you love her."

I'm reluctant to release his hand, but it's time.

I say goodbye to Imelda and my sisters, apologizing for my

rash behavior. I don't tell Piero I'm sorry. He deserved the punches he got. Then again, so did I. That's the Moretti way, I guess.

Back in the city, I walk to the café, but Colette isn't there. Nor is my mother.

I'm a fool to think Colette would have stuck around.

No, I'm an idiot for leaving her in the first place.

A couple walks arm in arm in front of me. The girl leans her head on his shoulder for a moment when they stop to browse a menu propped up on an easel outside a restaurant.

I remain at the café, waiting. Hoping. My phone beeps with a text from Colette. I jump to my feet. All she sent is an address north of here.

Back at the house, I grab a random set of keys from the peg by the valet—my father is known for his sports cars. In fact, he got started stealing cars when he was a poor teenager on the streets of Napoli. I click the fob once, twice. A Ferrari's lights blink.

"Perfect." I peel out of Naples and toward the address in a beach town called Sperlonga. It's the golden hour when I pull up in front of a café. The tables are empty outside and in. An old man stands behind the counter, his eyes wide like an owl.

"Is Colette here?" I ask in Italian.

He points toward the back room.

I find her sitting on an overturned milk crate, hands covering her face. Her back shakes with tears.

"Colette," I say, crouching beside her. "What's the matter? What happened?"

I gently take her hands from her face.

She looks up at me from tear-stained cheeks. Her freckles pop more than usual—must be the sun next to the sea. If she's surprised to see me, she doesn't show it.

"You happened, Antonio Moretti."

"I don't understand."

"There's nothing to understand. You told me to write a love letter to life, but I wrote one to you and I was mistaken."

My heart swells despite the accusation. "I'm sorry. You didn't make a mistake. I wrote a love letter to you too, but it got lost along the way." I draw her to standing. "Words don't quite properly capture how I feel, but I can show you in pictures."

"Show me what?"

I press my hand to my chest, mimicking one of the photos I took. "When I saw you that first time, it was like a lightning bolt struck me."

She shakes her head.

"Colette, *cuoro mio*. You are my heart."

The tears return.

"Why are you in here crying by yourself?" I ask.

"Because I saw that Catherine texted you where I was."

"Catherine?"

She explains that her friend was vacationing in Sperlonga. "She knew how I felt about you and sent that text. I just saw it."

"How do you feel about me?" I risk asking.

She looks up at me with watery eyes. "I love you."

"And I love you. From the moment we met, you spoiled me forever. There'd never be another woman like you. I sensed your heart was in pieces. I thought you needed tenderness and time. I also needed to prove to you that I could be the right man for you."

"More like a Romeo. You broke my heart."

"I'm sorry. I thought our love story was impossible. The business with my past and with my father needed to be resolved. I acted rashly. But there are ways to mend the heart and I plan to do everything I can to show you how sorry I am," I say. "I realize now that everlasting love is possible for me. Possible with you. For us." I tell her about going home, the fight with my brother, the talk with Imelda, and then the time with my father.

I meet her eyes and a long string of Italian words uncurl from my tongue. I kneel in front of her and repeat, "There has never been anyone, until now, who makes my heart want to rush from my chest and into your hands. Will you take my heart? Will you marry me?"

Her eyes sparkle and glitter.

She smooths a curl from in front of my eyes. "At the end of this trip, I wasn't sure what I'd find. It's silly, but looking back, I thought I'd discover parts of Marcus. But I collected pieces of us. I didn't find what I was looking for. Instead, I found you."

"Colette, all I know is it's true in every part of my being that I want to be with you and not leave it up to chance or fate or Cupid like you said."

She giggles.

"You are beautiful, clever, intelligent, funny, and sweet, you make me think and smile. I wake up wanting to be near you. I think about all of the food I want to cook for you so I can fill your heart-stomach. I want you to learn Italian so words will never fail us. I memorize your face, your arms, and your feet so I don't have to take a picture. That's what I know about love. And I know all of my love is yours if you want it."

She bounces on her toes, pulling me to my feet. "Yes, Antonio, yes."

She slings her arms around my neck and I kiss away the tears on her cheeks.

I whisper in her ear, "Let me love you. Let me make you happy."

We go through the backdoor and into the café and bookstore. The scent of paper and coffee beans makes me feel right at home, then I see a framed photo on the wall—one of my pictures.

"Where'd you get this?"

"I bought it from the AV Club. Never thought I'd see you again. Figured it belonged in my new café."

"Your café?"

"Catherine was going to buy it, but I needed a project. A place to land. Something to do. Turns out I love it here."

My eyes widen. "This is your café? Here, in Italy?"

She nods proudly. "Flavio is retiring. I can't seem to get rid of him though." She winks in the older man's direction. "He's showing me the ropes. But I still can't seem to make a good cup of espresso."

"I happen to know someone who can help with that," I reply.

She bumps my shoulder with hers. "I was hoping you'd say that."

"This place is amazing."

"I happen to think so. Though, I have no idea what I'm doing. Kind of like traveling. Learning as I go."

Dappled light reflects off the glass and I look up at a mobile hanging from the ceiling with various sized hearts covered in ink.

In Italian, the owner tells us those are love notes, hundreds of them, from customers over the years.

Colette's gaze meets mine. "Love is everywhere."

"Especially here," I kiss her on the cheek. "And here." I grip her ring finger. "Will you pick out a ring with me? I promise I'll purchase it properly."

She gives me a sideways look and we walk along the seashore as I explain about my family, our past and present. "My father was a thief. A playboy. He cheated in every sense of the word."

"I'm sorry, Antonio, but I have to say, wow. A real crime family?"

I wince at how that sounds.

"Things are different now," I assure her. "*Non sarà una spugna.*"

"What does that mean?"

"You will not be a sponge, tossed out with the dirty dishwater."

"You'll have to explain that one to me this time."

"It's an Italian expression whether you're a lawyer or a busboy. I got my first job outside the family doing dishes. As you can imagine by the end of the first night, I thought my arms were going to fall off. The boss was hard on me throughout the evening, telling me to work faster and so on. It was after midnight when the restaurant closed. I edged to the door, hoping I could finally go home and never return. He called me over. I worried I'd done something wrong, that I'd have to rewash all the dishes and glasses. With my head hanging, I returned to the kitchen."

Colette pinches my biceps. "I have a hard time believing these arms were sore."

I tip my head from side to side. "More like my pride. Anyway, the boss said to me, 'sit down, *gamberetto*.'"

"Wait. I know that one. *Shrimp.* I've been eating a lot of seafood." She gestures toward the row of restaurants opposite the beach.

"He was this hulking Neapolitan with a giant nose. Of course, I obeyed. He hollered at the sous chef who promptly appeared with two plates of warm pasta and fresh mussels. He told me to eat. I ate. I cleaned my plate before he did."

"The food here is so good, that's not hard to do. My food-heart has been very happy lately."

I chuckle. "He looked me up and down and asked, 'Are you a *spugna*?' I didn't understand. Am I a sponge? The grubby thing I was using all night to wipe the leftover food from the dirty plates? 'Of course, not,' I replied. I'll never forget anything about that night, but especially this, he said, 'Then don't let yourself get tossed out with the dishwater.'"

"Don't give up."

"Exactly. Never give up." I press my nose and forehead against hers. "I left you in a café. I found you here in one. I promise I will never give up on us."

Colette lifts onto her toes, kisses me softly on the lips, and says, "Neither will I."

I check my watch—a gift from my father for my eighteenth

birthday. The one I never took off…never gave up on him ether, in a way. "Hungry?" I ask.

"Always." Then she squeezes my upper arm again. "*Cozze*," she says. "Mussels. The ones in the shell."

My head falls back in laughter and I take her hand. "*Andiamo*."

CHAPTER 23
LOVE IS EVERYWHERE
COLETTE

Antonio and I spend the next weeks, nearly sleepless, as we clean up the bookstore, wait on customers, and restore order to Seaside Books and Coffee. There's also the second floor, jam-packed with stuff. But underneath it all, we find an apartment and office.

A strong sense of possibility and good fortune carries me through until the evenings when Antonio and I schlep upstairs. Only, it's not a cramped space, but a proper flat with a bedroom, bathroom, kitchenette, and the living room area serving as the office with a desk, books, papers, files, and supplies scattered everywhere.

"Welcome home," Antonio says each night.

It never gets old.

He parts the drapes framing the window and pushes it open, calling to mind the first night we spent together watching the sunrise. The brisk air makes goosebumps rise on my skin. Pockets of light shine on the water forming sparkly peaks. Over the roofs and across the river, there's a flickering on the horizon.

"Colette, you are my sunrise and my sunset."

"You are my sun and my moon."

Our eyes meet. He has a firm, but gentle grip on my hip and

then nudges me. Our chests press together, his arm pulls me closer, and words aren't necessary. It becomes about our bodies having a conversation as we kiss and kiss and kiss in that window bathed in city light and sunlight, basking in each other, and filled with so much possibility.

His hands smooth through my hair. Mine tangle in his.

He cups my jaw and I grip the back of his neck.

Our kiss deepens and I forget about the past, present, and future. What we have is right now, the big *this* as improbable and incredible as it seems.

It's not a fantasy. It's real.

How do I know?

By my racing pulse and Antonio's pounding heart as it presses against my chest.

The way my breath catches and how his turns heavy.

The gentle scratch of his stubble against my skin and the heat that builds on mine.

I don't have to worry about the kiss ending because our lives, together, are one long love letter.

Every day, we spend side-by-side, stealing glances and kisses. There certainly has been an uptick in customers since I started here. And an increase in our romance, torn from the pages of the best love story.

An impossible love story.

One that spans continents and miles and probability.

***

On a rare but drizzle day, my phone buzzes with a text from Catherine. I take a break from organizing the baking supplies.

Catherine: I'm the worst friend. I've been so busy that it's taken me forever to get these recipes to you, but you'll find them waiting in your inbox.

Me: You're a wonderful best friend. Thank you for sharing them with me. Just promise that you'll come back to Sperlonga soon. We're working on bringing some American flavor—cookies and hoagies—I'm calling it the Sperlonga Sandwich

Special. And life isn't the same without your grandmother's cookies. Hopefully, I can duplicate them.

Catherine: At this point, Hazel is probably the better judge.

Me: Remember when we went on the girls' trip to the lake? Maybe we can do that again but in Italy. Sometime after the wedding.

Catherine: I like the way you're thinking. Also, you'd better get your booty up here soon. I still want to take you to the shop for your gown. I cannot believe you're marrying a Moretti.

I send her a snapshot of the rock on my hand. I was right about Antonio. Even though when we met he worked as a busboy, the man has wealth on top of wealth, but this ring was purchased—I was there and saw the receipt. But we won't talk about that because when in Sperlonga...or Naples... Or Rome...

Catherine: !!! If you show that to Hazel, she'll be on the next plane to see that thing in person. It must weight ten pounds at least.

Me: Yeah, she'll be out here gloating. She's the one who forced me to take this trip.

Catherine: And look how well it worked out.

Me: Better than I could've imagined. Thanks again for making me stay.

Catherine: Thank Hazel for making you go.

Me: Group effort?

Catherine: Speaking of the lake, my cousin is still single. Does Antonio have any brothers?

Me: I thought she got married.

Catherine: The other cousin. The mean one.

Me: Actually, Antonio does have a brother. Piero. But he's mean too.

Catherine: They sound like they'd be a perfect match.

We send each other some cackling emojis and then I browse the recipes Catherine sent. I stash my phone when a customer comes in, but thankfully, Antonio waits on her. I get out the ingredients for the cookies. At the bottom of the recipe, Catherine's grandmother added, *When you mix in each ingredient, especially the chips, stir in a bit of love. You can't go wrong with love and chocolate.*

I bring Antonio a chocolate chip and pop it in his mouth. Nope. You can't go wrong with chocolate and love. I measure and cream, mix and fold. I give it my best shot, making a mess of the café counter and floor, but with each turn of the spoon, I stir in love, thinking of my friends, travels, and the man making espresso.

Flavio appears in the late afternoon, his smile a little higher today than yesterday. "Do I smell what I think I smell?"

"Chocolate chip cookies."

"Are they warm?"

"As if there's any other option."

"Is there milk?"

Antonio appears with three glasses and we sit at the table with a small plate of cookies between us.

Flavio takes a bite, sets the cookie on the napkin, and has a sip of milk. Then he starts laughing, a room-filling, chuckle.

My hands turn clammy and my throat thickens. "Did I add too much salt? Switch the sugar and baking soda? Do they taste like hubcaps?"

He gets to his feet and hugs me, still laughing before letting go, and declaring, "Love at first bite. These are rainy afternoons and warmth and plump grandmas. They are chocolate, buttery, sweet perfection—this shop will be just fine without me."

Relief sweeps through me and I look at Antonio, who's nearly cleaned the small plate of cookies I brought over. "Should I get more?"

His amused smile lifts his cheeks.

In the coming days, we don't see Flavio again. He must finally be enjoying his retirement and trusting that his labor of love is in good hands.

Whenever Antonio walks by, he nips a kiss on my ear. While

I'm mixing up a batch of cookies, he dips my finger in the bowl and then licks off the buttery dough. He doesn't let more than a few moments pass without reminding me how big his love is, for me, for the customers, for the scenery beyond the windows of the shop, for the dogs that come in thirsty from their walks.

His affections run deep, but I no longer need to be jealous or fearful of this Romeo. He just loves a lot, he loves big, and I understand how that kind of connection makes it so he's never lonely. I'm part of it, a big part of it.

I really am living my very own *Eat, Pray, Love* story—emphasis on the eating part. And the loving, especially. And I don't mind at all.

Weeks pass as we hustle to revive the shop. Every morning a line forms as people get coffee, pastry, and muffins on their way to work—Maxwell helped with recipes. Students fill the tables and study between classes. Writers disappear behind their laptop screens, and friends meet up in the afternoon for the Italian version of *fika*.

That night, while we make *panzanella* for dinner, and an Italian song croons from the radio, I have a brainwave.

"What if we took a page from the AV Club's book? If we hosted music or an open mic night. That kind of thing?"

Antonio and I are electric as we brainstorm. We have cookies and milk for dessert. I take a sip, purposely giving myself a milk mustache because I know he'll kiss it from my lips.

We plan for bands and book signings, coffee tastings, and art shows. And then there's the wedding. I've hardly had two seconds to think about that.

Especially as we get busier in the coming days, leading to our grand opening. But somehow I don't mind the exhaustion this time. Maybe it's because I'm fueled by kisses...and cookies.

All of those stolen glances, the times our fingers brushed, when he held my hand, it was all a prelude to this wonderful mix of romance and friendship, closeness and sweetness. Antonio's thoughtful in a way Marcus and all the other guys I ever dated never were. It surprises me because I'd all but convinced myself I'd never have this kind of connection with someone and I know it'll be forever.

We've more than made up for those missed kisses. Especially right now, during the afternoon lull. Antonio nips my ear with his teeth and then dives in for a mind-melting smooch.

A woman walks in and the bracelets around her wrist jangle.

I startle, launching myself backward.

Antonio's mother stands in the doorway.

"Don't break up the party on my account," she says, laughing. "I heard you were hiring."

Antonio staggers then glances at me, looking stricken, shocked.

I bite my lip. "I thought we could make this more of a family affair. Your mom has café experience."

Antonio's face falls and then brightens. "You arranged this?"

"When we went to Naples to visit your father last—I popped out for coffee. Kristy was working. I guess you could say I poached their best worker, but I don't regret it."

I get the first hug and then Antonio hesitantly hugs his mother. I know it'll take a while and probably a lot of trust-building, but I figure if Catherine can successfully get the love of my life back into my life, I can help restore Antonio's relationship with his mom. Or mum, as she says.

We've been texting a bit, mostly about the wedding. I have to prepare us all because the moment my mother finds out, she'll be on the first plane out of Charleston. There will be planning and purchasing and a lot of mom-zilla fussing.

I have to relish the laid-back Italian lifestyle while I can. Although, I didn't let Antonio return the Ferrari. Sometimes I like the fast lane too even if I'm typically more Fiat than a sportscar.

I'm sorting through some paperwork to properly arrange for my visa when Antonio appears and kisses my shoulder and then behind my ear. "I need you."

Butterflies do their DC-10 airplane thing—like the kind my dad used to fly.

Antonio kisses my chin and my cheek, meeting me back on the lips. "I need you downstairs," he says, smiling. "The audio people and the band are loading in for tonight."

Oh right, open mic night. "I almost forgot. I did forget. You've taken to this shopkeeper life. Thank you for sharing the load."

He stops me cold. "Colette, it's our love letter life. You're my inspiration. It's been you since the moment I laid my eyes on yours. Since I kissed your hand. I love everything about you. The way you sing while you bake. How you eat slowly, savoring. Laugh easily and long." He kisses me again.

I smile because I brought this wild, globetrotting Romeo to his knees. Tamed him. Showed him what love is. And he chose me. Every day, he reminds me of that.

I smile at the idea of him taking care of me, of the absurd possibility of getting married, of being loved. The word is on my lips. Love. An elegant L, a buoyant O, a V that's like an arrow to the heart, and a quiet E, because sometimes quiet is okay, necessary even.

"Somethings may be lost in translation. But not our love," he says.

Antonio kisses my nose and then my lips. And doesn't stop until someone hollers up from downstairs.

The rest of the evening passes in a flurry of preparation as we stow some of the books and make room for a crowd. We grind extra coffee and stock up for customers. Antonio hangs the photos of his latest project on the walls—it's part art showcase, concert, and cookie party.

People fill the bookstore and spill onto the patio. Antonio introduces the band, Mega. I knew he'd booked live music, but I figured it was someone local.

I mouth, *Seriously?* Because there's no way he'll be able to hear me over the chatter.

He winks and the band from London appears.

When the guitarist strums the strings and Misha starts singing, I suddenly feel warm all over, connected, plugged in, and complete. I'm part of this community: the big one in the world that took me across the Atlantic and through several cities and countries meeting all kinds of people along the way, but also to this smaller one here that we carved out of a failing coffee and book shop.

I snuggle closer to Antonio as we sway to the music. I finally found the opposite of loneliness and it isn't a word at all. It doesn't need to be. It's a feeling and at last, I'm living the truth of it. I've built bridges, often with help, and now I've crossed them and have connected with this tapestry of people and created a family.

By the time we're done cleaning up, it's late or early, I can't tell which. I'm not quite tired yet, still lit up by the excitement of the night—a massive success. Instead of stopping at the top of the stairs and going into the flat, Antonio opens a door opposite ours. Another stairway leads up and we take it to the roof.

The last of the warm summer night clings to my skin. With my hand in his, Antonio leads me to an open space near the edge of the roof.

There, cushions and blankets create a nest surrounded by flickering candles. At the center is a small cooler. I tilt my head, curious, but we remain standing and he points at the sleeping city. I'm awash with love for this place: the smells, the flowers, café, books, and people. I found my city, my street, my home.

"I have something for us." He opens the cooler, producing a small container. When he peels back the lid, the sweet smell of chocolate wafts. "Gelato."

He scoops a bite for me.

"This is what love tastes like and I love you," I tell him.

His smolder sparkles in the light of the moon. "I love you in English. *Ti amo,* in Italian. In Dutch, *ik hou van jou.*"

I feed him a bite of the chocolate gelato before it melts.

After Antonio swallows, he says, "In Danish, *jeg elsker dig* and Swedish, *jag älskar dig*. I loved you since the moment I saw you and carried that love with me through Amsterdam, on the train in Germany, across the ferry to Denmark, to Sweden, and all the way here. Oh and don't forget French, *j'taime*."

I kiss Antonio on the lips, tasting salt and chocolate and love. My heart moves closer to him at that moment as though magnetized by the invisible arrows of fate or whatever led us to be together.

"I love you, Antonio. I love this life." He kisses me again and I know that my heart is home.

EPILOGUE

The Lists

The Bucket List

London:

- Whitehall
- Buckingham Palace
- The Globe Theater
- The London Eye Ferris wheel
- British museum
- National gallery
- Westminster Abbey
- Saint Paul's Cathedral
- Prime Meridian
- Parks

Amsterdam:

- Canals
- House boats
- Floating flower Market
- Museums
- Cafes

Copenhagen:

- Check out Marcus's roots

Stockholm:

- Ditto

Paris:

- Croissants
- Baguette
- Pain au chocolat
- Cheese
- Macarons
- All the food!
- Oh, and the Eiffel tower

Love list

- Walk hand in hand down cobblestone streets
- Make a wish in a fountain
- He feeds you pastries or gelato or anything
- He helps older women in need of a strapping young man
- Is the perfect gentleman
- You laugh together
- He gives you the look (you'll know it when you get it)
- Generous with his time and attention

- He knows his way around the kitchen
- A romantic accent is preferable
- He reads, glasses a bonus
- When he looks at you, you feel like a ~~princess~~ queen

The *Why I Love* Antonio List

- His real name is Pinistro and he can laugh about it. Humor is key in a relationship.
- He cooks for me, nourishing my food-heart.
- The way he always reaches for my hand.
- He gets common American phrases wrong on purpose just so I correct him.
- His hands are works of art.
- His dark eyes rimmed gold.
- The tousled curls and stubble.
- The way he sees love everywhere.
- Life is an adventure with him.
- He's creative and kind.
- He's thoughtful and tolerates my silliness
- Then there's the smolder. Save me!

BOOK 5 SNEAK PEEK

Christmas is Coming!

Look for an Unconventional Christmas Romance, book 5, in the Falling into Happily Ever After series this holiday season.

Chapter 1: Minnie

On my Sunday jog through Central Park, I usually listen to a Disney movie soundtrack. But I need help to muster my Christmas cheer this year. A carol with lyrics about "Needing a Little Christmas" choruses through my earbuds, and I sing along. Loudly.

The pigeons, pecking something goopy and suspicious in a puddle, scatter. A woman walking her corgi gives me a look that's a cross between a scolding and a smile as I belt out the words—well, the ones I can remember while I interchange them with ones of my own.

I need something to make this cold morning run bearable.

I need someone special in my life and we're not going to talk about how his name is Tyler.

I need a little romance and a happily ever after.

Also, I could go for some chocolate, a chai, or a scone—rewards at the end of my run.

A man riding a bicycle and wearing an expression crimped with concern stops and assesses me.

As I pass, I say rapid-fire, "I need inspiration to present my village scene design to my boss tomorrow." Not that he cares.

Not that my boss cares either. Her soundtrack would be along the lines of the *Grinch Who Stole Christmas*. For the first time in my life, my merriment feels faraway like a seasick crocodile chomped down and swam off with it. It's not entirely my boss's fault, but something other than my lousy work situation and the unusual chill in the air feels different this year.

As I pound down the path, past dead grass, under the bare trees, and the bleak winter sky, I focus on the song lyrics. The reason for the season. The light and warmth and comfort despite the fact that inside, lately, I feel like I resemble these stark surroundings.

Exiting the park by my apartment on the Upper East Side, I enter my favorite bakery. It pumps out delicious smells but fails in the décor department. No garlands in the window or snowflakes dangling to imitate snow. Zero decorations. Then again, I haven't pulled out the red and green tubs from storage either. Maybe something keeps the holly, jolly on hold.

Sophie, the owner of the Honey and Lavender bakery and café, smiles when I come in. Without having to verbally place my order, in under two minutes, I have a warm spiced chai tea and a fresh cranberry walnut scone in hand. Yes, I'm a regular. Yes, I have a fondness for sweets.

I take a sip and bite while she rings me up. "The chai is always perfect, and this might be my favorite scone yet."

Her rosy cheeks lift with a smile. "You're the sweetest, Minnie."

"I'd argue those cinnamon rolls are the sweetest." I point to the tray in the display case with perfectly coiled confections drenched in glossy glaze.

My mouth waters, but I resist. In my head, Briony's voice comments about how my appearance reflects my sweet tooth. Unlike her, I'm not a toothpick.

Sophie chuckles. "As for the scones, I was torn between adding walnuts and almonds. Both are seasonal flavors. They each pair well with cranberries."

The woman is a baking master, rivaling Maxwell—Hazel's beau. I've never tasted something she made that wasn't delicious. "You can't go wrong, and I love the hint of orange."

She beams. "Wait until you taste what I have in store for the scones next week." She rubs her hands together. "By the way, did you get the approval from your boss?"

"Wish me luck. The presentation is tomorrow."

"I'm from a small southern town and while snow was seldom, I love your concept to recreate one of those charming Christmas villages but life-size." A timer dings and she remains in motion as we chat.

Comforting warmth like rubbing my hands over a fire fills me. "You can thank my aunt Vivienne. She was the queen of Christmas and had an extensive set of little houses, shops, and even a miniature ice skating rink. I haven't taken it out yet this year, though."

"I get it." Sophie spins her finger in a circle, indicating our surroundings. "I keep telling myself I'll get the decorations up, but each day seems to get away from me. Can't complain though. Business is booming, as they say."

"Doesn't it seem like time is flying? Hard to believe Christmas is in twenty-four days." I only know this because I have an app on my phone that reminds me, and not because I've been changing the numbers on my aunt's oversized Christmas countdown nutcracker. Nope. Haven't dusted that guy off yet.

"Sometimes I miss the slower, small-town pace back home. But the hustle and bustle of the city at Christmas is something special," Sophie adds.

I could stay and chat all day, but a line forms behind me. After stuffing a couple of dollars in the tip jar, I say, "I challenge us both to decorate by next Sunday."

"Challenge accepted," she says.

"And no making Teagh do it. That's cheating," I tease, referring to her flurry of pie orders last Fourth of July, resulting in him taking over decorating duty. The stars and stripes were a little askew, to say the least.

Sophie laughs. "He's not such a Grinch anymore, but he'd

probably just toss a little tinsel around and call it good. Don't worry, I won't let you down."

We share another laugh before I leave. I tuck the hint at a festive feel in my pocket because I'll probably need it later.

On my way home, I'm so focused on mentally rehearsing my presentation talk for tomorrow, I forget to cross to the other side of the street when I reach Madison and Sixty-First. Construction on the corner building has taken so long, you'd think they were building a pyramid or a massive igloo. I duck under the scaffolding, draped in massive sheets of protective plastic, and pass through a cloud of dust. I cough and blink rapidly until I'm in the clear. Sometimes I long for small-town life too.

Back at my building, I tiptoe past Mrs. Cricklewood's door and grip my keys so they don't jangle. My breath gets put on pause. I pray my door doesn't squeak.

Footsteps approach.

I struggle with the bolt lock.

Hurry, before it's too late, my inner voice commands. So much for the comfort and joy of being home.

Perspiration dots my forehead and it's no longer from my run through the park. The bag with the rest of my scone drops to the floor, scattering crumbs everywhere as the door across the hall opens.

A once-formidable woman with a voice to match glowers at me. "Young lady, what have I told you about being quiet?"

Yes, compared to her, I'm young. In my early thirties. But she was already old when I came to live here with Aunt Vivienne and has always terrified me.

I straighten. "I apologize, Mrs. Cricklewood."

"If this keeps up, I'll report you to the building super."

"You already did," I mumble. Three times.

The first infraction was when I had guests and yes, we were loud, but it was before nine p.m. and our game of charades was intense.

Another time I'd hung a cute Easter wreath with little plastic eggs and flowers on the door. Apparently, she's allergic to Easter or flowers—I'm not entirely sure.

Most recently, she took offense at the small group of friends I had over to watch the Thanksgiving parade. We didn't even make so much as a peep.

Ba humbug to her. Maybe that's why I haven't pulled out the tubs of Christmas decorations yet—I don't want to get cited and risk apartment building probation.

She looms in the doorway as if expecting me to defend my case, then eyes me more closely. "Why are you covered in white? Did you walk through a blizzard or something?"

I look down. White dust covers my black activewear. I try to explain that it was probably from the construction site, but she cuts across me.

"Didn't your parents teach you to wipe your feet before you enter a building?"

I stiffen at the mention of my parents as the old, familiar tension seizes my heart.

Glancing back, I left a trail of white footprints and a scattering of dust on the hallway carpet. As emotions well up, I'm torn between tears and a good, solid huff.

I draw a calming breath but start coughing again. Instead of the snappy retort on my tongue, the pause gives me a chance to offer grace as my parents taught me.

"Mrs. Cricklewood, I'm sorry about the mess. I'll clean it up and be more careful."

"Good,." She looks me over as if expecting me to argue. Then she gives a snobby sniff.

Aunt Viv used to call the people like her in the building who were rude *the Snooty Snob Mob*.

"Also, I'm going to the market this afternoon. Would you like me to pick up anything for you? I can also swing by the library. They recently extended their hours."

She crosses her arms and sniffs again. "I am an independent

woman. I can carry on with my own affairs, thank you very much."

I could reply with something like, *I know. I'm just trying to be helpful.* Or *I noticed you don't leave much anymore* (not once, to my knowledge, in the last week and counting). Or any number of sassy retorts, but I know how to deal with women like her. Silence is golden. Engaging with the grumpiness will only result in her raising objections, noting faults, and challenging my character. I've had plenty of practice with my boss, Ella.

A forced smile balances on my lips. "Very well. Let me know if you change your mind. Good day to you, Mrs. Cricklewood." I offer a friendly wave and secure myself in my apartment. I almost titter because my comment sounded so formal, like a character from one of my Regency-era romance novels, but Mrs. Cricklewood's comment about my parents snuffs out any laughter.

I've never been inside her apartment, but imagine it has a similar layout to my aunt's with an entry area that gives way to a large sitting room with oversized windows on one side and a hall to the kitchen and dining room on the other.

The décor in here is early twentieth-century classic but light and airy. Very little has changed since my aunt had the place updated when I was in my early teens, including my bedroom. I don't know if it was out of pity or guilt, but she had the interior designer give me a room fit for a princess complete with a four-poster bed, canopy, lacy curtains, and gilt furnishings. The old-world charm always made me feel like we lived in a fancy hotel or fairytale, even though my life was anything but. Well, post-accident. Before that, life was pretty great. Lately, I've been thinking about how much I lost.

After a shower, I pop my earbuds back in, not daring to incur Mrs. Cricklewood's wrath if I listen to Christmas carols over the regular speakers.

Reviewing the sketches for my presentation and running

through my presentation takes the better part of the afternoon. I don't stop until my phone beeps with a text.

Ty: What's cookin' good lookin'?

Me: Are you scavenging for food? It smells like Mrs. Cricklewood is making her weekly batch of hard-boiled eggs. You could probably knock on her door if you're hungry.

Have I ever complained to the building super about the sulfuric smell? No. But I need to get my angst out about how unfair she is somehow.

Tyler, my best friend, is the perfect balance of "I've got your back" and level-headed reason. He also has a top-notch sense of humor and definitely understands what we called the Cricklesnitch Sitch after my elderly neighbor complained about the "hoodlums and reprobates" I had coming in and out of the building. Yes, he often wears hoodies, but he's a professional photographer, millionaire, and has never been arrested—that I know of. Then again, he does venture to far-flung countries for extreme sports on the regular, so what happens in New Zealand, probably stays in New Zealand.

Ty: I'm afraid she'd try to poison me.

Me: Oh, come on. You're so charming.

Ty: Not even my smile works on her. I'd have to arrive armed.

Me: Speaking of arms, not the violent kind, I could use some muscle.

Ty: I'm your guy. He adds the arm-flexing emoji.

. . .

A long, unbidden sigh escapes. *If only.* If only he was *my guy* and not my best friend.

There's a pause in our messaging like we're both taking a breath. What do I say? *I wish...*

I made a wish once, and it went horribly, devastatingly wrong. So not that. Definitely not that.

My phone beeps again, tearing me from what could easily become a downward spiral of depression.

Ty: What do you need? Name your terms.

Me: Can I ply you with pizza?

Ty: I just got back from Italy. You'll have to do better than that.

Me: Takeout from the deli down the block?

Ty: What kind of labor are we talking about? Getting something off a tall shelf, repainting a room, or a complete kitchen remodel? I've created a system for payment. Pizza on the lower tier, five-course meal on the upper. I'm thinking Bonheur on Fifty-fifth if you want the diamond level kind of job.

Tyler's favorite French restaurant, also his last name. No relation. The French translation of *bonheur* is happiness. I think he likes the restaurant for that reason, and probably because it's where he takes his dates. An off-limits topic of conversation—we do not discuss our love lives, or my lack of one. He doesn't bring it up. I don't ask. But I do assume that they're all gorgeous and tall and as exotic as Ty's travels. In other words, nothing like me.

The doorman buzzes the intercom.

I startle.

The deep, male voice of the doorman says, "Miss Torsvig, Mr. Bonheur is here to see you."

That was fast.

I've told the doormen, Reginald and Wilber and Gregorio,

that they can always just let Tyler in, but they follow formality to the *T*—probably living in fear of Mrs. Cricklewood's wrath like I do.

But Tyler doesn't knock on the door...or text. Five minutes pass.

I check in with Gregorio—the weekend doorman. "Sorry, Miss. He got a message and hurried back outside."

My shoulders drop. Hot date? Emergency? Last-minute invitation to go white water rafting?

Me: Ty, everything okay?

Thirty minutes later...

Ty: Yeah. Sorry. Something came up. Talk soon.

My insides clench. Given the nature of my intense but secret crush on my best friend, my first thoughts are that he went to be with another woman. Someone prettier, cooler, and more fun than me. My second train of thought ventures toward the creative:

- He had to bail a friend out of a tight spot
- Photography opportunity of a lifetime
- Rescuing a kitten from a tree

All are somewhat reasonable. All have happened. Tyler is the kind of guy your parents want to call their son-in-law.

At the reminder of what I don't have, my thoughts turn darker. Toward the past. The last time I saw my parents was at Disney World. It was Easter...We went on an egg hunt. So fun. Truly the happiest place on earth. I've been searching ever since...

Looking for love.

For family.

To fill a void I fear I never will.

Mournful thoughts, an ache in my chest, and a loneliness I've only ever escaped when in Tyler's company carries me to the couch where I flick on Mary Poppins.

My aunt was a wonderful surrogate. She did her best. But I miss Mom and Dad every day.

I could need a little Tyler. Right this very minute.

Keep reading…

ALSO BY ELLIE HALL

All books are clean and wholesome, Christian faith-friendly and without mature content but filled with swoony kisses and happily ever afters. Books are listed under series in recommended reading order.

-select titles available in audiobook, paperback, hardcover, and large print-

♥

The Only Us Sweet Billionaire Series

Only a Date with a Billionaire (Book 1)

Only a Kiss with a Billionaire (Book 2)

Only a Night with a Billionaire (Book 3)

Only Forever with a Billionaire (Book 4)

Only Love with a Billionaire (Book 5)

Only Christmas with a Billionaire (Bonus novella!)

Only New Year with a Billionaire (Bonus novella!)

The Only Us Sweet Billionaire series box set (books 2-5) + a bonus scene!

Hawkins Family Small Town Romance Series

Second Chance in Hawk Ridge Hollow (Book 1)

Finding Forever in Hawk Ridge Hollow (Book 2)

Coming Home to Hawk Ridge (Book 3)

Falling in Love in Hawk Ridge Hollow (Book 4)

Christmas in Hawk Ridge Hollow (Book 5)

The Hawk Ridge Hollow Series Complete Collection Box Set (books 1-5)

♥

The Blue Bay Beach Reads Romance Series

Summer with a Marine (Book 1)

Summer with a Rock Star (Book 2)

Summer with a Billionaire (Book 3)

Summer with the Cowboy (Book 4)

Summer with the Carpenter (Book 5)

Summer with the Doctor (Book 6)

Books 1-3 Box Set

Books 4-6 Box Set

Ritchie Ranch Clean Cowboy Romance Series

Rustling the Cowboy's Heart (Book 1)

Lassoing the Cowboy's Heart (Book 2)

Trusting the Cowboy's Heart (Book 3)

Kissing the Christmas Cowboy (Book 4)

Loving the Cowboy's Heart (Book 5)

Wrangling the Cowboy's Heart (Book 6)

Charming the Cowboy's Heart (Book 7)

Saving the Cowboy's Heart (Book 8)

Ritchie Ranch Romance Books 1-4 Box Set

Falling into Happily Ever After Rom Com

An Unwanted Love Story

An Unexpected Love Story

An Unlikely Love Story

An Accidental Love Story

An Impossible Love Story

An Unconventional Christmas Love Story

Forever Marriage Match Romantic Comedy Series

Dare to Love My Grumpy Boss

Dare to Love the Guy Next Door

Dare to Love My Fake Husband

Dare to Love the Guy I Hate

Dare to Love My Best Friend

Home Sweet Home Series

Mr. and Mrs. Fix It Find Love

Designing Happily Ever After

The DIY Kissing Project

The True Romance Renovation: Christmas Edition

Extreme Heart Makeover

Building What's Meant to Be

The Costa Brothers Cozy Christmas Comfort Romance Series

Tommy & Merry and the 12 Days of Christmas

Bruno & Gloria and the 5 Golden Rings

Luca & Ivy and the 4 Calling Birds

Gio & Joy and the 3 French Hens

Paulo & Noella and the 2 Turtle Doves

Nico & Hope and the Partridge in the Pear Tree

The Love List Series

The Swoon List

The Not Love List

The Crush List

The Kiss List

The Naughty or Nice List

Love, Laughs & Mystery in Coco Key

Clean romantic comedy, family secrets, and treasure

The Romance Situation

The Romance Fiasco

The Romance Game

The Romance Gambit

The Christmas Romance Wish

On the Hunt for Love

Sweet, Small Town & Southern

The Grump & the Girl Next Door

The Bitter Heir & the Beauty

The Secret Son & the Sweetheart

The Ex-Best Friend & the Fake Fiancee

The Best Friend's Brother & the Brain

Visit www.elliehallauthor.com or your favorite retailer for more.

If you love my books, please leave a review on your favorite retailer's website! Thank you! xox

ABOUT THE AUTHOR

Ellie Hall is a USA Today bestselling author. If only that meant she could wear a tiara and get away with it ;) She loves puppies, books, and the ocean. Writing sweet romance with lots of firsts and fizzy feels brings her joy. Oh, and chocolate chip cookies are her fave.

Ellie believes in dreaming big, working hard, and lazy Sunday afternoons spent with her family and dog in gratitude for God's grace.

Let's Connect

Do you love sweet, swoony romance?
Stories with happy endings?
Falling in love?

Please subscribe to my newsletter to receive updates about my latest books, exclusive extras, deals, and other fun and sparkly things, including a FREE eBook, the *Second Chance Sunset*!
Sign up here: www.elliehall.com ♥

facebook.com/elliehallauthor
instagram.com/elliehallauthor
bookbub.com/authors/ellie-hall

ACKNOWLEDGMENTS

To all the cozy chair, the corner of sofa, by the fire, lying in bed, by the pool, curled up somewhere quiet "book" travelers out there, I hope this story brought you a few moments of excitement, escape, and enjoyment. I appreciate those of you who read, review, and share my books and am so glad we're on this journey together!

Printed in Great Britain
by Amazon

26620769R00138